Gemima, Speedy, Pauli Peanuts
and Other Visitations
from Ray Muggles

Gemima, Speedy, Pauli Peanuts and Other Visitations from Ray Muggles

Ray Muggles

Copyright © 2023 Nigel Barrett

The moral right of the author has been asserted.

Apart from any fair dealing for the purposes of research or private study, or criticism or review, as permitted under the Copyright, Designs and Patents Act 1988, this publication may only be reproduced, stored or transmitted, in any form or by any means, with the prior permission in writing of the publishers, or in the case of reprographic reproduction in accordance with the terms of licences issued by the Copyright Licensing Agency. Enquiries concerning reproduction outside those terms should be sent to the publishers.

This is a work of fiction. Names, characters, businesses, places, events and incidents are either the products of the author's imagination or used in a fictitious manner. Any resemblance to actual persons, living or dead, or actual events is purely coincidental.

Matador
Unit E2 Airfield Business Park,
Harrison Road, Market Harborough,
Leicestershire. LE16 7UL
Tel: 0116 2792299
Email: books@troubador.co.uk
Web: www.troubador.co.uk/matador

ISBN 978 1805140 658

British Library Cataloguing in Publication Data.
A catalogue record for this book is available from the British Library.

Printed and bound in Great Britain by 4edge Limited
Typeset in 11pt Minion Pro by Troubador Publishing Ltd, Leicester, UK

Matador is an imprint of Troubador Publishing Ltd

For all the great short story writers. Thanks so Much.

Contents

Gemima	1
SOMEONe To LEAn On	17
mR StINkY pANtS	37
Speedy and the Shattered man	63
esme	119
THE CONFESSION OF PAULIE PEANUTS	143
Don't talk about your semen in front of my friends.	209
HESTER CLUTTERS' WAITING ROOM	233

Gemima

(On December 26th 1908, in Rushcutters Bay, Sydney, Australia, Jack Johnson defeated Tommy Burns to become the first black heavyweight boxing champion of the world).

December 28th

Mary Lou was four and whispering secrets to her friend Gemima. She didn't want her brother Tommy to hear, and had her mouth close to Gemima's ear.

Until someone abruptly bumped her.

Making her glance up.

Tommy had vanished; she couldn't see him anywhere.

Looking nervously around, she saw people stampeding past, some yelling and shouting.

"Tommy?" she called, afraid.

Giant bodies flashed past her.

"Tommy?" she called again.

The choking dust was so thick now it was like early morning fog.

"Tommy?"

As loud, angry voices closed in around her, she still couldn't see Tommy.

Or her Ma.

Or Pa.

She gripped Gemima's hand tighter.

"TOMMY?"

Confused, she stood gazing around.

Somebody crashed into her, knocking her over.

Her hand slipped from Gemima's as she fell, her cry smothered under her tumbling body. She rolled and came to rest, coughing up dirt, shocked.

"Oh my, oh my," a voice lamented above her.

A towering stranger blocked the light and reached down for her.

She stared up at him, dazed.

"Forgiv' me littl' missy. I surely am sorry."

His hand clasped her and gently lifted her to her feet.

"Yoo 'kay littl' missy?"

"Gemima?" she whispered.

"Huh? Nuthin' broke?"

She slowly shook her head.

"Yoo'll have to forgiv' a clumsy ole fool. Sure yur 'kay now little missy?"

"Where's Gemima?" Mary Lou asked softly.

He was older than her Pa, she noticed; had a greying beard and a straw hat pushed back on his head. The hat had a white feather sticking out of it. Something was perched on his shoulder, something long and metal. Confused by it at first, she suddenly recognised it.

It was a photograph taking machine.

She'd seen one once in the town. A man stood it on three legs, put his head under some cloth, held up something in his hand, and after it popped, smoke flew up into the air.

"Huh?" he grunted.

He looked her up and down, appraising her, then glanced impatiently over her head, peering at something beyond.

"Whats ya name little missy?"

"Gemima," she mumbled.

"Huh? Gemima. Well, I'm rul sorry Gemima."

He reached into his waistcoat.

Plucking something out of his pocket, he said,

"Take this here card littl' missy and I'll give a couple or two complimentary foty-graphs fuh ya fam'ly.

He pushed the card into her little hand.

Mary Lou accepted it, still too dazed not to.

He smiled kindly, tipped his hat to her with a little bow, and looked again off into the distance.

Looking back at her, he said,

"Be sure un give that there card to ya Pa now, little Gemima, an I'll getcha them foty-graphs."

She watched him walk away, one arm clutching the picture machine, steadying it on his shoulder, heading toward a crowd that had gathered under the trees.

She looked around for Gemima.

"MARY LOU!"

Her brother Tommy was running toward her.

"I tol' yuh stay close by me Mary Lou," he scolded her.

He sucked in a distressed breath through his teeth. "Look a'the mess all on yuh new dress. Wait'll Ma sees. She gonna tan your hide fur sure."

"A man knock me over," she sniffed.

Tommy began brushing dust off her dress with his hand.

"New dress Ma store bought special," Tommy mumbled as he did his best to erase the dust and dirt.

"I've lost Gemima," Mary Lou told him, not caring about her dress, looking around.

Everyone seemed to be under the trees now. There was uproar over there.

"Yuh face too!"

Tommy licked his finger the way he'd seen Granny Louella do, wet her face, and scrubbed at the brown on her pale face with his shirtsleeve.

"Gotta find Gemima," Mary Lou told him.

"Huh?"

"Gemima."

He tutted. "We ain't got no time tuh look fur her."

Mary Lou couldn't bear the thought of Gemima lost, and all by herself. "I wan Gemima."

"We'll find her later," he snapped irritably. "Look yonder Mary Lou," he pointed over at the trees, bursting with excitement, at the noisy herd under its bows, "they're fixin ah lynchin."

Mary Lou wasn't listening. She just wanted to find Gemima, and resisted at first when Tommy yanked at her.

"Come on Mary Lou," he snapped angrily, "we'll miss it."

She had one final, quick scan for Gemima before yielding to Tommy's tug. They trotted off toward the trees. Stopping a short distance from the commotion, they stood watching.

Mary Lou's eyes widened with bewilderment.

She recognised the women clustered around in a group, in their best bonnets and dresses, fanning themselves as they chatted and pointed. She saw her Ma amongst them, with all her Aunts and her Granny Louella too.

Beyond them, under the trees, were the men.

They scared her.

She didn't even recognise them at first.

Didn't realize they were her uncles and neighbours.

Hank Garvey, their nearest neighbour but one, looked so crazed.

"Look Mary Lou, there's Pa," said Tommy, pointing.

But was that her Pa?

In the centre of the group, there he was, but he looked so different from her usual gentle Papa, his face red and contorted.

She watched him tugging and tugging at something. She'd never seen her Pa so furious, not even last year when Tommy almost burned the barn down.

He gave another angry heave at something, and then she saw what her Pa was yanking at.

An apparition popped up from the scrum, his arms waving.

It was an old darkie.

As Pa yanked again, the old, grey haired darkie screamed.

Mary Lou winced.

Pa dragged the struggling old darkie across the dirt as the other men kicked and punched him. Mary Lou watched his face turn bloody and wet.

Then she saw another.

This second darkie was much younger than the first.

And Mary Lou knew him.

He was her friend.

...one day last year, in early summer, Mary Lou and Gemima had been wandering near the creek when a bee stung her arm. When she burst into tears, a Negro boy fishing

nearby had dropped his pole, come running over, and tended her throbbing arm with all kinds of plants he plucked from the ground, speaking gently to her, reassuring her, calming her down, and she'd felt much better. He'd even walked them part of the way home.

Everyone called him Feather, he'd laughed, 'cos I light as a feather,' and he was, she saw, small and bony.

He had a gap in his front teeth when he smiled, his teeth white against his black skin.

She'd seen him numerous times since then at the creek. He'd even shown her and Gemima how to use his fishing pole and the best bait to use for tempting catfish.

The last time she'd seen him, just a few days before, he parted from them with a grin and a wave.

Why was he here?

"HEY TOMMY!"

Tommy and Mary Lou saw Lee Diddel and his little brother, Sam, scampering toward them.

Tommy knew they'd jaw about Johnson beating Burns.

Heck, everyone was talkin' about it.

"Wait'll the niggers hear bout this," Lee Diddel said breathlessly, stopping, "they won't be so big in their britches bout Johnson for long."

"Johnson cheated," Tommy said with great authority, "Pa says he hit Burns low and cussed out his wife while he wus doin it."

"Johnson's the Devil," Sam Diddel piped up, parroting what he'd heard his Grandad Morton say.

"Pa says this-the worst day for the South since we lost to those Yankees in 65; says every white man gonna remember this day with shame in his heart."

"Pa says it weren't right no white man fightin' no nigger in the first place," Lee added.

"That's why they had to fight in such a Godforsaken place like Aust-tralia," Tommy told Lee, remembering his Pa saying it, and that word, and how he liked the sound of it. Godforsaken. "They'd never allowed it no place else."

Lee liked the sound of that word too. Godforsaken. It tumbled around in his mind until he remembered a better one. Old Man Tucker had said it just half an hour ago, shaking his head, Infamy.

That's what he'd said.

He shook his head like Old Man Tucker,

"Infamy. A day of infamy," Lee said, "That's what it is," said it just like Old Tucker did.

"Where's Ostralia?" asked Sam Diddel.

Lee tutted in disdain and gave his brother a shove, "Don't yuh know nuthin?"

Tommy told them, "Pa says Aust-tralia's the asshole of the world. Ain't got no streets there or nuthin."

Mary Lou wasn't listening.

She was watching Feather.

He looked petrified.

She couldn't understand why anyone would be angry with him, why anyone would want to hurt him.

The men swarming around the diminutive, bony black figure reminded her of that pack of starving wild dogs she'd seen last wintertime near the chicken coop. Pa had shot some of the snarling critters with his shotgun before they ran away.

Feather's shirt was ripped off. She watched his skinny arms, the same skinny arms that had been so kind to her, trying vainly to ward off blows and kicks. He fell to the floor and she saw Hank Garvey kick him in the teeth. Her Pa grabbed Feather by the wrist, snarling and shouting at him.

Mary Lou lifted her arm, pointing, her mouth hanging open. *They didn't understand who Feather was.* He was her friend. They *shouldn't do that.* Her Pa shouldn't be so angry with Feather…

She pointed but no one noticed.

"Johnson won't be champ long. Wait till Jeffries comes outta retirement," Lee Diddel said.

"Jim Jeffries' rip Johnsons arms off. Lick him good," Tommy agreed.

"Pa says Jeffries' the greatest pugilist ever lived. He's the real champ," Lee said.

"Jeffries' make sawdust outta Johnson," Sam Diddel added.

Tommy and Lee laughed.

"My Uncle says Jeffries' made of iron," Lee told Tommy.

"An he's bored just tendin' to his alfalfa fields. He's ah itchin to wipe that grin offa Johnson's face. Pa says how he heard tell Jeffries already in trainin', an he's gonna meet Johnson the second he steps off the boat from Austtralia and knock him back into the ocean right infront of everybody," Tommy lied. His Pa hadn't said anything of the sort.

"My Grandad says Tommy Burns nuthin' but a runt anyways," Lee countered, "never was a proper heavyweight in the first place."

"Now he's shamed the white race," Tommy repeated what he'd heard said so many times that day.

Mary Lou watched.

In his desperate attempt to escape, Feather tore her Pa's new Sunday best white shirt, soiling it with his blood.

She pointed again. *Stop hurting Feather*, she wanted to tell them, but her mouth just hung open silently.

"Cos o'that runt Burns the white race livin' in shame," said Lee, echoing another of his Grandad Morton's opinions.

"Jus fur money, too. Pa says Burns bad as Judas Scariot. Gettin' paid his thirty pieces o' silver."

"That's wot Burns got paid in Australia?" Lee asked.

"They got no dollars in Ostralia then?" Sam Diddel wondered.

Lee shoved his little brother. "Course they don't got dollars in Australia. That's why they pay em in silver, dummy. Don't yur know nuthin?"

"Pa says Aust-tralia brung shame on the world. Johnson's in all the dailies now."

"Johnson's the Devil," Sam Diddel piped up again.

"Now the niggers gonna be all uppity. Thinkin' Johnsons the President or something. Gotta put 'em in their place, Pa says," Tommy told them, "right quick."

"Look," Lee exclaimed excitedly, "they almost got the rope ready."

"Niggers ain't so tough now," Tommy grinned.

Mary Lou watched the older darkie crying pitifully as his wrists were tied behind his back and a noose tightened around his neck. He started yelling, cursing through his tears. Suddenly, he was yanked off the ground, his feet kicking, his face unable to breathe. Hank Garvey secured the rope and the old darkie swung in the air, his legs kicking frantically.

"Come on Tommy, let's get closer," Lee cried in excitement.

Tommy glanced down at his little sister. "Nah," he said in disappointment, "gotta mind Mary Lou."

Tommy remembered the last time he'd neglected minding her. He'd got distracted playing with Billy Bob Miller and Mary Lou had wandered off and got lost for hours. Tommy got whupped good that night and didn't want to be again tonight.

"Ah, come on Tommy," Lee cajoled, "she'll be okay."

"Nah," Tommy shook his head, "Pa be riled if I don't watch her. She's already wandered off."

"Come on," Lee shoved his little brother Sam, and they hurried off to get closer.

Tommy looked down at his little sister.

"Why you always gotta wander Mary Lou?" he complained.

Mary Lou didn't answer.

She was watching the lynching, her arm out, pointing, tears rolling down her face.

Tommy frowned. "They're just niggers Mary Lou. Ain't nuthin to be cryin' bout."

Mary Lou watched Hank Garvey slip a noose over Feather's head while her Pa tied Feather's hands behind his back.

Poor Feather was crying, his face a gruesome mess.

Her Pa heaved on the rope and Feather lifted into the air, his legs kicking.

Mary Lou watched him dangle and twitch and swing, sobbing.

"Wait til Johnson hears bout this," Tommy said eagerly.

They stood watching as Lee and Sam Diddel clambered up on the bodies, clutching onto the hanging men's legs, and began to swing back and forth.

Tommy groaned in disappointment. He wanted to go over there and play too. He glanced down at Mary Lou.

"Mary Lou, let's go play on the niggers," he suggested hopefully.

Mary Lou shook her head.

"Come on, Mary Lou," Tommy pleaded, yanking her hand.

Mary Lou shook her head, dug in her heels.

Tommy recognised that pout and knew she wouldn't budge now.

"I wanna go play with Lee," Tommy told her, "promise yuh won't wander Mary Lou. Promise me?"

Mary Lou watched Lee Diddel and his brother Sam swinging on Feather's legs, laughing.

Except it wasn't Feather anymore. That ghoulish, broken thing hanging there had a purple face, horrible bulging white eyes and its tongue, its huge red tongue hung out of its mouth.

That wasn't Feather. Feather had been beautiful.

She wanted him back.

Her Pa was drinking with Hank Garvey, the two of them touching glasses.

"Don't go wandrin' Mary Lou," Tommy snapped at her, "stay put. I'll be watchin, hear?"

He ran off, glaring a final warning over his shoulder at her, and joined Lee and Sam, swinging on the legs of the hanged men, giggling.

Mary Lou watched as the men and women, uncles and aunts, neighbours and strangers, mingled again, drinking and chatting and eating.

What had happened seemed like a horrible dream.

…except for the two apparitions hanging there, and her Pa's ripped, bloody new shirt…

She saw the man then. The one who'd knocked her down.

He'd taken the photograph taking machine off his shoulder and had set it up on the ground; three long, thin legs, a box on top, cloth hanging down; pointing it at the hanging men in the trees.

He tried to shoo her brother and the Diddels away from the hanging men, but every time he did and went back to his camera, they returned and swung on the dead men's legs again.

Mary Lou remembered what he'd said about giving her some photographs and glanced at the card still clutched in her hand.

She looked again as, having given up on moving the troublesome boys, the man's head disappeared under the cloth, and he raised something high in the air. It flashed and gave off a puff of smoke.

Mary Lou dropped the card onto the floor.

Desperate to find Gemima, she wandered off.

Still sobbing, she searched and searched. She knew Gemima would be just as upset as her when she found out about Feather.

They were friends too.

But Mary Lou couldn't find her anywhere. She was lost. A dread grew in her belly; maybe she wouldn't see her ever again.

Then she spotted her.

At a sprint, she rescued Gemima from the long grass and dirt. She'd been trampled and was streaked with mud.

"Oh Gemima, are yuh o-kay?" she asked.

Mary Lou tried to tell her about Feather, but could only sob in her ear.

She hugged her doll tight to her chest, weeping.

SOMEONe To LEAn On

Amelia heard the doorbell.

It must be Barbara...

They sat next to each other in class.

Funny, she hadn't been expecting her.

It'd be nice to see her though.

Perhaps they could go to the High Street and look around the shops. *She still had some pocket money left...*

The doorbell chimed again.

Amelia stood, slowly, pressing both hands flat on the soft, padded chair arms, her eyes fixed on the object hanging there. She knew its name. It was a – a – damn –

She grabbed it, knowing she couldn't walk without it, even if she couldn't remember its name. It fitted her hand like a glove, yet felt repugnant. *Imagine what Barbara would say when she saw it...*

Amelia hoped Barbara wouldn't mind her taking it with them when they went browsing.

She shuffled as fast as she could but the front door seemed a long way.

As she got closer, the letterbox flipped open.

"Amelia?"

Panic overwhelmed her. She stared at the eyes peering at her through the letterbox.

That wasn't Barbara.

She'd been expecting her friend Barbara.

"Amelia?"

Disorientated, Amelia began to shake. Fear pounded through her.

"Amelia?"

She went to the door and in a shrill panic, asked, "Who are you? What do you want? Where's Barbara?"

"It's Rachel, Amelia. Open the door."

"I certainly will not," Amelia snapped.

"I've come to give you your tea," the eyes said.

"What?"

"I've come to give you your tea."

"You've what?"

"OPEN THE DOOR Amelia."

"I will not," Amelia snapped.

"Amelia," the eyes sighed wearily, "Amelia, I DON'T HAVE MUCH TIME. I'm already running late. Please OPEN THE DOOR."

"I certainly won't open the door. I'll call the police if you don't go away."

The eyes tutted and vanished. The letterbox clattered closed.

Amelia could feel her heart racing. She hoped whoever it was would go.

The letterbox opened again. A hand poked through holding something in its fingertips.

"Amelia, Amelia, look at my I.D. It's RACHEL. I'M YOUR CARER. I'M here to make you a SANDWICH AND A CUP OF TEA."

Amelia peered at the laminated badge and vaguely recognised the photograph.

It was Rachel.

"IT'S RACHEL AMELIA."

"I know who you are," Amelia snapped irritably.

The hand vanished from the letterbox. The eyes appeared again. "Could you open the door Amelia?"

"Alright, alright."

Amelia didn't want a carer; didn't need one.

Somewhere buried in a fog, she recalled an argument about the whole thing with someone. Someone had *made* her take on a carer.

Forced her.

"Alright, alright," she unlocked the door.

A blast of freezing cold air made her recoil and shiver.

"It's cold out there today," Rachel said as she stepped inside, "Sorry Amelia."

Amelia stared hard at the stranger following in Rachel's footsteps.

Rachel took off her coat.

"This is Cassy. Remember I told you she'd be with me today?"

Amelia didn't like strangers in her home, so if she'd been told about it, she'd certainly have remembered.

"You did not," Amelia corrected her.

"I did mention it last time. Perhaps you've forgotten," Rachel said, hanging up her coat.

Amelia bit her tongue and said nothing. She hadn't forgotten. What cheek!

"Hello Amelia," Cassy smiled, holding out her hand.

Amelia ignored the hand. "Who are you?"

"Hang your coat there," Rachel told Cassy softly.

"Cassy," Cassy answered, pulling her arms from the

hooded, heavy coat.

"Who?"

"Cassy," she repeated, a little louder this time.

"Lassy?"

Amelia noticed them glance at each other with amused smiles.

"CASSY," Rachel repeated, "have you got your AID SWITCHED ON Amelia?"

"Cassy?" Amelia repeated, "Cassy? What kind of name is that?"

"I'm on holiday NEXT WEEK Amelia. Remember I told you. Cassy's GOING TO BE COMING TO LOOK AFTER YOU WHILE I'M AWAY. I'm SHOWING HER THE ROPES today."

"I don't need anyone coming here next week, or any other week," she snapped sternly.

"Come and sit down Amelia. COME BACK INTO THE WARM."

Rachel touched Amelia's elbow and gently guided her back into the living room. It was warm and stuffy in there with the gas fire on. The news on the television had subtitles appearing and disappearing on the bottom of the screen.

"SIT YOURSELF DOWN now, and I'll GET YOU A NICE CUP OF TEA," Rachel said, settling Amelia into her chair. "Let me take YOUR WALKING STICK," Rachel took it and hung it off the chair arm.

Amelia stared at it.

So *that's* what it was; that's what it was called.

A walking stick.

"Who's that?" Amelia asked.

"That's CASSY," Rachel told her.

"What does she want?"

"She's GOING TO LOOK AFTER YOU."

Amelia was outraged. "I don't need anyone to look after me."

"She's going to be here NEXT WEEK Amelia, while I'm ON HOLIDAY."

"But why?"

"To get you a CUP OF TEA and a SANDWICH and CHECK YOU'RE OKAY."

"I don't need anyone checking up on me."

Rachel glanced at Cassy, arching her eyebrows. She'd warned her about Amelia.

Wheels were already in motion to put Amelia in a home. It wouldn't be long now.

"We've been through this before Amelia," Rachel reminded her charge, "YOU KNOW you have to have SOMEONE LOOKING IN ON YOU EVERY DAY."

"Fiddlesticks," snorted Amelia.

"And WHILE I'M AWAY, CASSY WILL BE POPPING IN TO SEE YOU."

Amelia snorted again. Pushing both hands down on the chair arms, she began slowly rising to her feet.

"Where ARE YOU GOING NOW Amelia?" Rachel asked.

Amelia froze, half standing, looking at Rachel and Cassy blankly.

"SIT yourself BACK DOWN, AMELIA," Cassy coaxed her, stepping closer.

Amelia stared fiercely up into Cassy's eyes, then lowered herself slowly back into the cushion.

"Let me show you the kitchen," Rachel said softly to Cassy.

She touched Amelia's arm. "I'll GET YOU A CUP OF TEA."

They went into the kitchen.

Amelia frowned, staring at the television. She didn't recognise the presenter reading the news. Didn't know what they were doing in her kitchen. She glanced at the – what was it called? – hanging off the chair arm. Damn it, damn it, damn and blast it…

Slowly, she pushed herself to her feet, took 'the thing', off the chair arm, and began shuffling toward the kitchen.

She stopped in the doorway and saw strangers kneeling on the floor, plundering her cupboards.

"What on earth do you think you're doing?" she demanded to know, shocked.

"I'm just showing Cassy where everything is kept Amelia."

"What?"

"I'M JUST SHOWING CASSY WHERE EVERYTHING IS KEPT."

"What's it got to do with you?"

"Why don't you go and SIT DOWN, Amelia, and we'll bring you a cup of tea."

"I don't want to sit down."

"We'll bring you a nice cup of tea."

"What are you doing in my cupboards?"

"Getting YOUR TEA READY Amelia."

The kettle bubbled and clicked off, filling the corner of the kitchen with steam. Amelia wondered why it hadn't whistled.

"Come and SIT BACK DOWN AMELIA," Rachel said, cupping Amelia's elbow gently in her hand. Amelia let herself be led slowly out of the kitchen.

Then she stopped abruptly, scowling intently at the wall.

"What have you done with the stairs?" she darted a bewildered look at Rachel.

"You don't have stairs Amelia."

"What?"

"You DON'T HAVE A STAIRCASE IN YOUR FLAT AMELIA."

"No staircase?" Amelia clucked. "Of course there's a staircase. It was here a minute ago. What have you done with it?"

"You're thinking of your old house. YOUR OLD HOUSE HAD A STAIRCASE."

Rachel put a little pressure on Amelia's elbow to try and get her moving, but Amelia wouldn't budge.

"You'd better put it back before my father notices it's gone. He'll have your guts for garters."

That was one of her mother's favourite reprimands, 'your father'll have your guts for garters my girl.'

Amelia didn't like it. She never had. She thought it sounded common. Talking about guts.

"He'll have your guts for garters," she repeated.

"Shall we SIT YOU DOWN and get that cup of tea Amelia."

Amelia glanced into Rachel's eyes, looked down at her feet, and began to shuffle forward again.

"What WOULD YOU LIKE IN YOUR SANDWICH Amelia?"

Rachel led her charge back to the chair. Amelia slowly lowered herself and sat.

"What would you like in your sandwich Amelia?"

"Pardon?"

"WHAT WOULD YOU LIKE IN YOUR SANDWICH?"

"Sandwich?"

"There's CHEESE AND TOMATO, or there's that bit of HAM FROM YESTERDAY."

"Yes."

"CHEESE AND TOMATO?"

"Ham."

"YOU WANT HAM?"

"Yes, cheese tomato and ham."

"Okay, SIT TIGHT, Amelia. I won't be long."

A stranger appearing in her house had unsettled Amelia. She felt restless.

Hands she didn't recognise twisted in her lap; claws covered in unsightly brown blotches.

Amelia glanced around.

Where was Barbara…

She'd gone to the door and let Barbara in, she knew.

Perhaps Barbara would know what had happened to her hands…

Amelia slowly pushed herself to her feet, staring at 'the thing' hanging off the chair arm, anger bubbling inside her because she couldn't remember its name.

Barbara would know…

Amelia shuffled across the room thinking perhaps Barbara had gone upstairs to the toilet.

Bathroom.

She corrected herself immediately.

Bathroom.

She hated people referring to the bathroom as the toilet, yet there she was, doing it herself.

"Bathroom," she muttered.

Perhaps Barbara was upstairs in the bathroom…

When she glanced up the stairs for some sign of Barbara, she froze in horror.

The *stairs were gone. There was just a wall…*

Something clattered in the kitchen.

Perhaps Barbara was in the there helping her mother make the tea…

"What on earth do you think you're doing?" Amelia snapped at them from the doorway, "what are you doing in my kitchen."

"MAKING YOUR SANDWICH AMELIA," Rachel said over her shoulder, smearing margarine over a slice of bread.

"Who are you?"

"It's RACHEL, Amelia."

"Where's Barbara?"

Rachel came over and began walking her back into the living room.

"BARBARA'S NOT HERE AMELIA."

"But she was just here," Amelia protested.

"I think you're getting MIXED UP AGAIN AMELIA."

"But I just let her in."

"THAT WAS US YOU LET IN."

Amelia frowned. She didn't believe it. She'd just *seen* Barbara.

Rachel settled Amelia in her chair.

Cassy appeared with the finished sandwich on a plate and waited a moment while Amelia got comfortable.

"There you go sunshine," Cassy placed the sandwich on the chair arm.

Amelia scowled up at Cassy, glanced at Rachel, and then at the sandwich.

"How bout A BICCY WITH YOUR CUP OF TEA?" Cassy asked.

Rachel frowned. Cassy was one of those carers who sometimes lapsed into babyspeak with clients. She didn't like it.

"Or a sweetie?"

Amelia glanced sharply at Cassy. "I beg your pardon?"

"Would YOU LIKE A SWEETIE?"

"Who on earth do you think you're talking to young lady? I'm not a child. Sweetie indeed!"

Cassy glanced at Rachel, pulling a mock expression of horror. "Sorry Amelia."

"I was a teacher for over forty years," Amelia told her.

"Oh, you were a teacher?"

"YOU WERE A HEADTEACHER FOR AWHILE, WEREN'T YOU AMELIA," Rachel added.

"I was a teacher for over forty years," Amelia repeated, "sweetie indeed."

"I'm sorry Amelia," Cassy apologised again.

Rachel tipped her head at Cassy, indicating she should sit and chat to Amelia.

She wanted Amelia to become as familiar with Cassy as possible in the short time they had. Even though she knew Amelia would probably have forgotten Cassy by the next visit. But that couldn't be helped.

"Eat your sandwich Amelia," Cassy coaxed, perching herself on the sofa opposite, her elbows on her knees.

Amelia fixed Cassy with an angry glare. Cassy shifted back on the ample cushion under its force.

Rachel went to fetch a cup of tea.

Amelia studied the sandwiches on the plate. They'd sliced them into squares instead of triangles, and cut the crusts off. She hated that.

"So, you WERE A TEACHER AMELIA?" Cassy asked, trying to get Amelia to like her.

"I was a teacher for over forty years," Amelia answered, picking up one of the squares.

"What did you teach?"

Amelia bit the corner off the square. As she chewed she realized how hungry she was.

"WHAT DID YOU TEACH?"

Amelia glared.

This portly young woman was irritating her. She hated eating and talking at the same time. She chewed silently.

"Amelia taught history," Rachel said, coming back in with the tea.

"History? You could help my youngest, Amelia. He's just starting history in school."

Rachel put the cup and saucer (Amelia didn't like mugs) onto the little coffee table near Amelia's chair.

"What YEAR DID YOU TEACH?" Cassy asked.

"Amelia was a secondary school teacher. SHE TAUGHT THE BIG KIDS," Rachel answered in proxy.

"The teenagers," Cassy added.

"She taught in some pretty ROUGH SCHOOLS IN LONDON, DIDN'T YOU AMELIA?"

Amelia swollowed.

"It wasn't easy trying to teach the history of the industrial revolution to the deprived inner city, I can assure you," she told them.

The two carers glanced at one another. It was always a little startling when the old Amelia broke through.

Amelia picked up the paper tissue next to her plate and daintily dabbed the corner of her mouth. She furrowed her brow, holding it out, staring at it.

"I wonder what that is?" she scowled. "It's not got a name. It's quite nice. It's quite handy, isn't it?"

"It's a tissue," Rachel told her.

Amelia peered at Rachel in disbelief.

"IT'S A TISSUE, AMELIA."

"A tissue?" Amelia barked.

Rachel tapped Cassy's knee with her fingertips, tipping her head toward the kitchen. The two of them left Amelia nibbling her sandwich.

When they returned, Rachel held two small plastic beakers containing Amelia's tablets.

"Amelia?"

Amelia had finished her food and was engrossed in the television.

"AMELIA?"

Amelia glanced at Rachel, then at Cassy. "Who's that?" she asked.

"CASSY. HERE'S YOUR TABLETS."

Amelia frowned at the beakers. "What tablets?"

"YOUR TABLETS."

Amelia didn't like taking her tablets. "I don't need tablets."

"You know you do Amelia. Doctor's orders," Rachel pushed one of the beakers into Amelia's gnarled hand.

Amelia gazed into the beaker. "How many are there? I can't take all these."

"ONLY THE SAME AS ALWAYS."

Amelia stared unhappily into the plastic beaker. Rachel handed her her teacup.

"HAVE A SIP OF TEA."

Amelia popped a tablet into her mouth and washed it down with tea.

"AND THE NEXT ONE."

Amelia did it, pulling a face. Rachel took the empty beaker off her and gave her the second one, glancing at the carriage clock on the mantelpiece. She had six other appointments to see before ten. She couldn't afford to run over time with Amelia.

"I'll be rattling soon," Amelia answered.

"How about a CHOCOLATE BISCUIT?"

"Yes please," Amelia answered.

Rachel went into the kitchen, put two chocolate biscuits on a plate, and returned to the living room.

Cassy was perched on the edge of the sofa chatting to Amelia. Amelia was ignoring her.

Rachel hoped everything would be okay next week while she was away.

"I was just asking Amelia IF SHE HAS ANY CHILDREN," Cassy said to Rachel.

"Of course I don't have any children," Amelia snapped irritably.

Rachel put the biscuits on the chair arm. "You have A DAUGHTER, AMELIA," she reminded her.

Amelia shot her a startled look.

"YOUR JESSICA."

Amelia glared.

"You've a daughter CALLED JESSICA?" Cassy asked.

"REMEMBER YOUR DAUGHTER JESSICA?" Rachel asked.

"Of course I remember Jessica," Amelia spat contemptuously. "Do you think I'd forget my own daughter?"

Rachel glanced at the time again. They still had to get Amelia into her nightie and dressing gown.

"Eat YOUR BISCUIT Amelia."

Amelia looked at the biscuits and slowly picked one up. "I've still got all my own teeth you know," she said to Cassy.

"I wish I did Amelia," Cassy replied, "look at this."

Cassy opened her mouth and pressed her finger against one of her front teeth. The tooth slipped down, exposing a gap. Cassy jiggled it up and down.

Amelia blinked, startled. "Good god," she gasped.

Rachel laughed.

"Look at this Amelia," Cassy jiggled it some more.

Amelia couldn't believe it. "Good god."

"I lost that when I was fifteen, Amelia. Got knocked out by a hockey stick."

"A what?"

"A HOCKEY STICK. DURING A HOCKEY MATCH."

Amelia was appalled. "A hockey stick?"

"It was Tina Ford. She said it was an accident but I still think she did it deliberately. HIT ME RIGHT SMACK IN THE FACE SHE DID AMELIA."

Cassy jiggled the tooth a bit more for effect, her mouth hanging open.

Amelia glanced at Rachel with distaste. Rachel hid her amusement.

"Tina Ford never did like me Amelia. She liked me even less when I poached her boyfriend in the second year.

She ended up moving to MILTON KEYNES and getting divorced."

"Who moved to Milton Keynes?" asked Amelia.

"TINA FORD."

"Who?"

"SHE'S THE ONE KNOCKED MY TOOTH OUT."

"Well, I've still got all my own teeth," Amelia told them.

"YOU HAD THE GOOD SENSE NOT TO GET HIT IN THE GOB WITH A HOCKEYSTICK AMELIA. Accident my foot," Cassy added, running her tongue over the still smarting wound.

Rachel glanced at the clock again. Time was pressing.

"Let me show you the bedroom," Rachel said to Cassy. "YOU FINISH YOUR TEA Amelia. I'M going to show Cassy where your bed things are."

"Pardon?"

"I'M GOING TO SHOW CASSY WHERE YOUR BED THINGS ARE."

"Back in a jiffy," Cassy told Amelia, following Rachel.

Amelia frowned, watching Cassy hitch up her trousers as she left the room. They were far too tight for her. She watched the empty doorway.

She put her empty teacup back on the saucer.

Where was Barbara? She couldn't understand where she had got to...

Amelia slowly stood up, glancing around. *Her mother would want some help in the kitchen. Amelia wondered why she hadn't called her...*

Amelia was not, absolutely not, going to have balloons at her party... She'd told her father she was too old for balloons...

As she shuffled down the hall she noticed the bedroom

door ajar and the light on. She pushed the door open and was terrified to see two strangers picking through her mother's belongings.

"I'll call the police if you don't leave," she warned them.

"IT'S ONLY US AMELIA," Rachel said.

"Those are my mother's things. What do you think you're doing?"

Rachel came over and put a reassuring hand on Amelia's shoulder. "It's Rachel, Amelia."

"I know who *you* are. Who's that?"

"CASSY Amelia."

"Remember, with the tooth," Cassy reminded her, jiggling her tooth again.

Amelia stared at her dumbfounded.

"DO YOU NEED THE BATHROOM AMELIA?"

"Yes."

"Come ON THEN," Rachel led her toward the bathroom.

Amelia wouldn't accept any help, she knew, so Rachel let her go in alone. "DON'T LOCK THE DOOR AMELIA, WILL YOU?"

Amelia flashed vexed eyes at Rachel as she closed the door. Rachel heard the lock click and groaned.

"Of course she's locked it," Rachel said quietly in exasperation. Last time Amelia had locked the bathroom door, it had taken twenty minutes to get her out again.

"Has she locked it?" Cassy asked from the bedroom doorway.

"I'll do the washing up and then come back and see if she's finished."

When Rachel came back and knocked on the door, there was no response.

"AMELIA?"

She knocked again. "Amelia?"

"Who's there?"

"RACHEL, AMELIA."

"Who are you?"

"OPEN THE DOOR, AMELIA."

"What do you want?"

"It's RACHEL."

There was no response.

"AMELIA?"

"Leave me alone."

"IT'S RACHEL."

"Go away."

"YOUR CARER."

"Whoever you are, go away."

"AMELIA, OPEN THE DOOR."

"My father will be home any minute."

"WE NEED TO GET YOU INTO YOUR NIGHTIE, AMELIA."

"My what?"

"YOUR NIGHTIE."

"I don't know you."

"YES YOU DO AMELIA. IT'S RACHEL."

"What are you doing here?"

Rachel sighed. Cassy was watching from the bedroom doorway, smirking. Pulling her I.D. badge from her pocket, Rachel bent down and slipped it under the bathroom door.

"I'M PUTTING MY I.D. BADGE UNDER THE DOOR AMELIA."

Rachel waited. After a few moments, the lock clicked and the door moved. Rachel glanced at Cassy in relief.

Amelia shuffled into view.

"ARE YOU OKAY?" Rachel asked.

"I'm perfectly fine," snapped Amelia angrily.

"We need YOU IN THE BEDROOM AMELIA."

Amelia, heading for the living room, stopped, looking around in confusion.

"WE NEED YOU IN THE BEDROOM AMELIA."

"The bedroom?"

"WE NEED TO GET YOU INTO YOUR NIGHTIE".

"I don't need any help getting into my nightie. The very idea," Amelia snorted.

"You know you do Amelia, AFTER THAT FALL YOU HAD."

"Poppycock."

But she let herself be gently guided into the bedroom, until she saw the stranger, standing by the bed, smiling at her, and stopped dead in her tracks.

"Who on earth are you?"

"Cassy. It's CASSY, Amelia," the stranger said.

"Where's Barbara?"

mR StINkY pANtS

ernie heard his mother talking about mr stinky pants again. only she didn't call him mr stinky pants. she called him mr bishop.

"poor old boy," she said.

"awful, isn't it?"

"and he hasn't a soul in the world. not a soul."

"not a soul."

"and he isn't saved."

"no. he isn't. isn't saved."

the echo was brenda trattle. who lived on the landing below. and generally agreed with his mother about everything. brenda trattle and his mother worshipped at the church around the corner together.

ernie was on the floor playing with his cars. his postman pat van was being carjacked by a gang of minis. (they were the baddies, and terrorised all his cars.) he paused the robbery and looked up.

his mother was sitting in her favourite lounge chair, dressed in her dark purple flower dress. she had a cup and saucer of tea on the chair arm. her thick, long legs were stretched out in front of her, crossed at the ankles. her slippers were worn out. her rich chocolate complexion shone in the light.

she was big. his mum. a big mum.

or maybe it was that mrs trattle, dressed in a bright white cardigan, sitting opposite his mother nursing a cup and saucer on her knee, perched on the edge of the sofa, was so little. short and oh so thin. his mum said she ate like a hamster. there was a small plate next to mrs trattle with a large chunk of home made sponge sitting on it. ernie's mum always gave brenda something to eat when she came around, to try and, as she put it, 'put some feathers on her bones,' even though brenda always said she didn't want anything.

"now don't forget your cake brenda," ernie's mum reminded her neighbour, nodding at the plate on the sofa arm.

mrs trattle's small glasses flashed at the cake. "you always give me such a huge piece joy."

ernie's mother tutted. "huge? brenda? i don't think anyone else would think that was huge."

ernie thought it was. brenda gave the cake further dubious scrutiny.

"can i have it if she doesn't want it?" ernie piped up.

both turned to him.

"of course you can't," his mother snapped irritably, "that's brenda's piece of sponge cake. brenda is our guest. you don't eat a guest's sponge cake when a guest is kind enough to come around and visit. you should know better than that ernie. "

"but she doesn't want it."

"of course she wants it," his mother answered.

"but she isn't eating it."

"she'll eat it when she's ready to eat it. don't interrupt ernie. it's not polite."

"it's alright," mrs trattle cooed.

"it's not alright. he has to learn. go back to your cars ernie."

ernie scowled at them.

"i brought a piece of sponge to poor old mr bishop afterward," ernie's mother said, turning her attention back to mrs trattle, "and it was a bigger piece than that. he wolfed it down," she added in partial reprimand.

"probably starving, poor old boy."

ernie's mum's face fell.

brenda hadn't meant it to sound like that and quickly asked, "so what time was it?" and then buried her face in her cup.

ernie's mother took a sip of tea and put the cup carefully back on the saucer. "well, i'd just left to go to work, so just about five. it was still dark. it was freezing brenda. poor thing. i noticed all the commotion as soon as i got into the high street. just outside the dry cleaners."

"oh, there," brenda murmured.

"police cars, an ambulance – "

"i don't know how you do it?" brenda interrupted.

"what?"

"get up at four o'clock in the morning."

ernie's mother gave brenda a look. "i don't have much choice brenda. needs must."

"of course."

ernie's mother gave a little shake of her head. brenda had an annoying habit of interrupting.

ernie continued watching brenda trattle's piece of sponge with great concentration.

"poor old boy," brenda sighed.

"he's not a boy," ernie piped up.

four eyes snapped onto him.

"he's an old fogey, " ernie explained to them, "not a boy."

"he is *not* an old fogey," ernie's mother told him firmly, "that's a very rude thing to say."

"that's what they call him," ernie answered.

"who's they?"

ernie was thinking of jasmine next door. kai at the end. they called him an old fogey. and worse. but he didn't tell.

"huh," his mother said with scorn, as if that had put him in his place.

brenda trattle peered at him blankly.

"i don't want to hear you referring to mr bishop as an old fogey. that's rude. do you understand ernie. he's not an old fogey."

"but she called him a boy. and he's old."

his mother sighed deeply. "if you mean brenda, say mrs trattle, or brenda, not *she*. brenda isn't the cat's mother. say *brenda* called him a boy."

"i know she did. and he's not a boy."

"it's just an expression," brenda said softly.

"yes," ernie's mother glanced from brenda to ernie, "it's just an expression. it doesn't mean he's physically a boy."

"what's wrong with calling him an old fogey?"

"it's not polite. that's what's wrong with it. it's rude. isn't it brenda?"

brenda didn't look certain but agreed. "yes."

ernie didn't mention that they all called him mr stinky pants as well. he knew his mother would be angry. they'd all seen him walking around with his trousers covered in poo.

"go back to your cars ernie," his mother snapped.

ernie didn't move. mrs trattle still hadn't touched her cake. ernie's mother noticed ernie staring at it, licking his lips.

"eat your cake brenda," she ordered bossily.

"oh, joy," brenda sighed, as if she felt sorry for her.

"i don't like to see good food wasted."

ernie didn't either.

"anyway, brenda, there he was, poor old boy, in his slippers and pyjamas, with the police there. i thought there'd been an accident. i crossed the street on my way to the bus stop wondering what was going on and then saw poor old mr bishop."

"in his pyjamas?"

"in his pyjamas brenda."

"poor old boy."

"he looked very distressed brenda."

"did he?"

"i don't think he had a clue where he was."

"oh."

"not a clue what was going on."

"who called the police?"

"i don't know brenda."

"what's going to happen to him joy?"

"i suppose he'll have to go into a home."

mrs trattle sipped her tea and shook her head. "poor old boy."

"when i saw it was him, i went over and asked this policewoman what was wrong," ernie's mother continued, "slip of a thing she was."

"what was he doing?"

"poor old mr bishop?"

"yes."

"just standing there. this young policewoman was asking him questions. trying to ask him questions anyway. he didn't have a clue brenda."

"terrible."

"so i explained to this young policewoman that he was my neighbour. she asked me if i knew what he was doing wandering around at night in his pyjamas. so i explained to her, about, you know, poor old mr bishop's mental faculties; how he's gone downhill recently."

"oh, he has, and so quickly."

"very quickly. very quickly, isn't it brenda."

"hard to believe."

"so i explained all that to this policewoman. know what she asked me brenda?"

"what?"

"she asked me if he had alzheimer's."

"oh."

"so i said i wasn't sure. what do you think brenda?"

"most likely."

"there he was brenda, poor old boy, in the street, shivering. i felt so sorry for him. he looked absolutely lost. so helpless he looked brenda. like a lost little boy."

"dear, dear."

"then the ambulance driver wrapped him in a blanket."

mrs trattle suddenly picked up her spoon and scooped a bit of sponge into her mouth. she put the spoon back, dabbing the corner of her mouth with a tissue.

ernie's mother paused a second, watching her, then snapped out of it.

"this policewoman brought me over to him, and, oh, you know what he did when he saw me brenda?"

"what?"

"he hugged me brenda."

"oh. did he?"

"hugged me and started crying. and you know the problems i've had with him in the past. hugged me brenda."

"oh. the poor thing."

"and he was shaking. all skin and bone. all skin and bone."

"oh, joy."

"they asked me if he had any relatives they could contact. but there's no one is there?"

brenda shook her head slowly. "no one i know of."

"and then they wanted me to go to hospital with him."

"did they?"

"but how could i? i had to go to work. and you know what they are. if i don't go to work i don't get paid. you know what mr chatterjee's like. he's not going to care. all he cares about is whether those offices get cleaned or not. he gave me a hard time about being late as it was."

"did he?"

"oh, yes. a little hitler he is sometimes. i explained it all to him but he wasn't interested. all he cares about is that agency and making money. i'm afraid," ernie's mother paused, twisting her teacup in the saucer, looking into it. "i wish i could have gone to the hospital with him. i wish i could."

"but how could you joy?"

she looked at brenda. "exactly. how could i brenda? how could i? this little policewoman gave me such a look when i said i couldn't go. such a look. but how could i brenda? i had to get to work. then i've got to get home and give ernie his breakfast. it's all very well expecting people to do these things. i do my best brenda. you know i do."

"oh i know."

"i said i'd go along later and see how he was."

"it's good of you to do it joy."

"they put him in the ambulance and took him away. and guess what brenda?"

"what?"

"he was back before i was."

brenda tutted.

"no beds."

"no beds," brenda repeated sadly.

"nothing wrong with him physically, see, brenda. nothing wrong physically. it's his mind. it's his mind that's the problem. so they sent him home. said he'd be better off in his own home."

"i wonder if the army had anything to do with it?"

ernie's mother scowled. "with what?"

"his mind going."

"why would the army have anything to do with it?"

"well, he was in the army for years, wasn't he?"

ernie's mother took a sip of tea and cleared her throat. "i don't see how serving in the armed forces could have anything to do with the onset of dementia, brenda."

"you're probably right."

"it could happen to anyone."

"i expect. i suppose he is better off in his own home though," brenda said.

brenda could be very vexing to ernie's mum at times.

"but for how long brenda? it can't go on can it?"

"no. no it can't."

"it can't go on."

"what about social services? a home help?"

"home help?"

"will they give him one?"

"but he needs full time care brenda. it's no good someone popping in twice a day. what good is that? he needs full time care."

"think they'll put him in a home then?"

"what else can they do?"

"and he's always been so independent, poor old boy."

"who's home?" ernie piped up.

"never you mind," his mother told him, "no one is talking to you."

mr stinky pants was going away somewhere?

"why is he going to a home?" ernie asked.

"he isn't well," mrs trattle answered softly.

"so he's goin to hospital?"

"if you mean mr bishop, ernie, then say mr bishop."

"mr bishop."

"that's better."

"so he's goin to hospital?"

"no," ernie's mother answered, "he isn't going to hospital. he'll probably go to a special home for elderly people who need looking after."

"who looks after them? will his mother look after him?"

"mr bishop is far too old to have a mother ernie."

"will his granma look after him?"

"if mr bishop is too old to have a mother, ernie, then he's too old to have a granma."

"who'll look after him then?"

"nurses," mrs trattle answered.

"nurses and doctors?"

"yes."

"but you said he wasn't goin to hospital."

"why don't you play with your cars ernest?" his mother suggested irritably.

ernie glanced with disinterest at his cars. "will we go and visit him when he's bein looked after by doctors and nurses?"

brenda glanced at ernie's mother.

"would you like to go and visit mr bishop when he's in a home being looked after by doctors and nurses ernie?" his mother asked.

ernie hadn't thought about it properly before. he frowned. he wasn't sure he would like to visit mr stinky pants, so he said nothing.

"ah hah," his mother said with finality, as if that had put him in his place.

"poor old boy," brenda sighed.

"he'll be better off in a home, brenda."

"i suppose. long as he's looked after properly. you know what some of these homes are like, joy."

"what else can they do brenda?"

"oh, i know."

"what else can they do?"

"such a shame."

brenda peered at the carriage clock on the mantelpiece.

"well, i'd better be going joy," she said suddenly. "randall will be back soon."

ernie's mother shot a frown at the uneaten piece of sponge on the sofa arm.

she noticed ernie grinning expectantly.

"you've left your sponge brenda."

"you always give me such a huge piece, joy."

ernie got to his feet, eyes locked on the sponge.

"i'll see you sunday, if not before," brenda said to ernie's mother, heading for the door.

"god willing," ernie's mother answered.

ernie's mother opened the door for brenda.

"give randall my best," she said as brenda went outside onto the cold balcony.

"i will," brenda wrapped her cardigan tightly around herself, "oh, it's bitter."

she waved and hurried off down the landing, her heels clacking on the concrete.

ernie's mother closed the door, shaking her head. "that woman tries my patience ernest, but she's a good woman. a good christian woman."

"can i have her sponge?" ernie asked.

his mother tutted. "no, you may not have her sponge."

she lunged for the sponge before ernie could and plucked it up off the chair arm.

ernie moaned angrily.

"gluttony is one of the seven deadly sins, ernest."

"but she left it," he protested.

"you already had sponge today ernie."

"but i thought you didn't like to waste good food," he reminded her.

"huh," she responded, "sharp as a pin, i'll give you that. i hope you put as much of that into your schoolwork and your bible studies."

ernie frowned. "what do you mean?"

"you know what i mean," she answered.

he did too.

she carried the sponge into the kitchen. ernie followed her.

"you're not throwing it in the bin?" he cried shrilly.

"of course I'm not throwing it in the bin. i do not waste good food. especially not food i've made with my own hands. you should know better ernest."

she put the sponge down on the worktop and studied it a moment. he watched, his eyeline just high enough for him to see what she was doing.

taking a knife from a drawer, she cut off the tip of the sponge, mumbling, "hardly touched it," shaking her head.

ernie frowned. "so you're eating it?"

"no," his mother answered, "i'm not eating it. i'm giving it to mr bishop."

mr stinky pants?

"that's not fair. he already had cake today."

"i'm sure he'd appreciate another slice."

"why can't i have another slice then?"

"mr bishop is bigger than you. he can handle two slices. and he's got no one to look after him. that's why. enough ernest."

ernie frowned, realizing he wasn't going to get the piece of sponge. not when his mother used that tone.

she wrapped the cake in a white plastic bag.

"come with me ernie."

they went outside. his mother pulled the door closed after them. ernie shivered.

"it's cold," he complained.

"we won't be long," she told him.

"i wanna stay here."

"you're coming with me. we'll be back in a minute."

she grabbed his hand and yanked him.

they lived on the second floor. there were four flats on their landing. mr stinky pants was at the far end. ernie could hear kids playing football in the playground below. he could see grey sky. dark clouds moving quickly over the dirty city buildings.

they got to mr stinky pants door and found it open. ernie's mother pushed it and peered inside. her voice taking on a strange, high pitch, like she was singing a hymn in church. "mr bishop? mr bishop? are you there? mr bishop?"

no one answered.

both of them took a few tentative steps inside, peering around the messy flat. ernie had never seen such a tip. it was cluttered and filthy. ernie wrinkled his nose at the sour smell.

there were photos on the walls of someone in an army uniform. lots and lots of photos. someone vaguely familiar. it was him, ernie realized. mr stinky pants, young and polished, smiling and strange. photos of him with his arm around other soldiers. in one of the photos, he was sitting on a tank and it was sunny. in another he was standing stiffly saluting, sergeants stripes on his arm. in another photo he was lying back, gripping a machine gun, grinning. in another he was holding up a funny drink containing fruit in a big glass, dressed in a bright yellow flowery shirt…

"mr bishop? mr bishop? hello."

she let go of ernie's hand. "wait here," she told him.

she went from room to room, holding the sponge in her hand, "mr bishop? mr bishop? hello?"

finally she stopped outside the closed bathroom door and tapped on it with a looped finger. "mr bishop? hello? are you in there? mr bishop?"

she opened the door, a deep frown cutting into her face at whatever she saw, but it was empty of mr stinky pants.

she came over to ernie. "where on earth can he be?"

"he's out."

she tutted. "yes, thank you ernest. but out where? and why was his front door open?"

she dragged ernie back outside into the cold. walking quickly, still holding the plastic bag containing the sponge, she looked out over the concrete balcony wall.

ernie gazed at her in bewilderment when she let out a little squeal.

"there he is. there he is," she exclaimed, looking down. "MR BISHOP. MR BISHOP. MR BISHOP. HELLO!" she called out.

ernie snatched his hand out of hers, scampered to a nearby plant pot, and stepped up onto it to see over the wall.

"HELLO MR BISHOP. MR BISHOP HELLO," his mother shouted.

ernie could see mr stinky pants below. he was dressed in light blue striped pyjamas and red slippers. he was shuffling along, but stopped when he heard his name, looking around.

"MR BISHOP. MR BISHOP. HELLO."

mr stinky pants swivelled his head around, confused, hearing his name but unable to see who was calling him.

"oh dear," his mother sighed, "MR BISHOP, HELLO, MR BISHOP."

mr stinky pants seemed to be getting more bewildered down there, twisting and looking.

"oh dear, oh dear," his mother sighed.

"why's he in his pyjamas?" ernie asked.

"wait here ernest," his mother snapped, waving a long brown finger in his face. "you wait here, do you hear? wait here."

he nodded.

ernie watched her hips bouncing as she hurried away.

he peered over the wall.

mr stinky pants was wandering away now. after a minute, he saw his mother trotting after him across the tarmac, still holding the cake aloft.

"mr bishop. mr bishop. hello."

he stopped and turned.

ernie watched his mother go up to him, clasp his arm gently with her hand, and talk into his ear. she was taller than him. he was stooped and thin and had a grey beard. she began leading him slowly back toward the stairwell. behind them, beyond a high steel mesh, a group of the estate kids were noisily playing football in the playground. no one took any notice of mr stinky pants and his mum. after awhile, they disappeared from ernie's view.

he waited, shivering, wanting to go home, but too afraid to move because his mother had told him to wait. he stood staring out over the buildings. flecks of rain began falling from the dark, ominous sky.

finally he heard voices. he watched his mother and mr stinky pants emerge from the shadows at the far end of the landing.

"…get you indoors mr bishop. you'll catch your death of cold," he heard his mother saying. "it's bitter. you should have a coat on; why haven't you got a coat on mr bishop?"

"i have," he muttered.

they came nearer.

"i'm supposed to be meeting someone," mr stinky pants told her, "meeting someone you see. that's why i've got my coat on."

"but you haven't got your coat on mr bishop."

"haven't i?"

"no. and you'll catch your death."

he glanced at her. "huh? but i'm supposed to be meeting someone you see."

"who are you supposed to be meeting?"

bewildered, he asked, "who?"

"yes. who?"

mr stinky pants glazed eyes suddenly alighted upon ernie. he stopped, pointed at ernie, and said, "what's he doing here?"

"that's my son, ernest."

mr stinky pants stared at ernie with dazed wonder.

"i haven't seen him since rhodesia."

ernie's mum glanced into ernie's bewildered face, and tugged gently at the old man's arm.

"let's get you in out of the cold mr bishop. get you a pullover."

but mr stinky pants wouldn't budge. he stared at ernie as if he'd seen a ghost.

he pointed at him again. "he used to get my tea."

"no mr bishop."

he turned and looked at her.

"that's my son ernest."

he was confused. "your son?"

"that's right. my son. ernest."

"your son? so you're from rhodesia."

"no. we're not from rhodesia. and it's zimbabwe now, mr bishop."

"huh?"

ernie's mother moved her mouth closer to his ear. "it's zimbabwe now, not rhodesia."

mr stinky pants gestured aggressively. "zimbabwe?" he spat the word in disgust. "what a dogs dinner they've made of it over there. zimbabwe my fuckin' arse."

ernie's mother drew herself erect in indignation. "i'll ask you not to use profanity in front of myself and my son, mr bishop."

mr stinky pants glared back at her, unrepentant.

she gave his arm another gentle tug. "let's get you inside mr bishop, before you freeze to death."

he lurched after her, his slippers shuffling on the concrete.

"i am cold," he said, shrivelling suddenly, "i am cold."

"course you are. you didn't put your coat on. you've got goose pimples mr bishop."

as they passed ernie, mr stinky pants, his head twisting sideways, gave him another lingering glare.

"he used to bring me my tea in rhodesia," he repeated, "i knew his mother too."

"i'm his mother, mr bishop."

confused, he replied, "you?"

"let's get you home mr bishop."

ernie trailed them as they slowly got closer to mr stinky pant's flat.

"what about my meeting, though?" mr stinky pants asked, stopping.

"who are you meeting?"

"i don't know."

ernie's mum raised her voice a little and said into his ear, "i don't think you have a meeting mr bishop. i think you're confused."

"oh, i do," he insisted gently, shuffling over the threshold into his flat.

she closed the door behind them.

"let's sit you down and get you a nice cup of tea. wouldn't you like a hot cup of tea. it'll warm you up. wouldn't – wouldn't you like a cup of tea?"

"oh yes," he answered, looking from her to ernie. "is that why the tea boy's here? i'll show him."

"and a slice of sponge," she added, waving the white plastic bag under his nose.

mr stinky pants was still staring at ernie.

his voice took on a harshness that scared ernie. "lazy. lazy they are. got to put a stick across their backs sometimes. that's the only cure. the lazy little fuc – "

"a piece of home made sponge with your tea mr bishop?" she interrupted shrilly.

his eyes locked onto the bag ernie's mother was flying under his nose.

his eyes lit up. his voice softened. "oh. i like sponge."

ernie could see something icky on the back of mr stinky pants pyjama bottoms but was afraid to say anything.

ernie's mother led mr bishop toward the living room.

"now you sit down in the warm."

ernie thought mr stinky pant's flat was just as cold as it was outside.

"i'll put your sponge out and make you a nice cup of tea."

"oh, thank you. thank you."

"you've got to stop wandering off mr bishop."

"i don't wander.

she guided him into the living room.

"you have a tendency to wander mr bishop."

ernie had never seen a place so filthy and messy. newspapers and magazines all over the furniture and floor. piles of dirty clothes everywhere.

"dear dear," ernie's mother said softly, taking it in.

ernie wrinkled his nose at the pungent, sour smell.

she led mr stinky pants to the sofa, and as he turned around to sit, she noticed the stain on the back of his pyjama bottoms.

"oh no, no. wait. wait mr bishop," she cried in alarm.

he'd started to lower himself but she yanked at his elbow.

"wait a moment, mr bishop," she all but shrieked, "wait!"

he abruptly stood erect again, bewildered.

"am i getting sponge then?"

"yes. mr bishop. first we need – oh dear – we need to go into the bathroom for a minute. you've, um, oh dear – come with me, come this way mr bishop."

still holding the plastic bag containing the sponge aloft, she led him toward the bathroom.

"ernest, take this," she snapped.

ernie took the bag from his mother.

"put it in the kitchen. i'm taking mr bishop into the bathroom. you wait here. don't touch anything ernest. you hear me? don't touch anything."

"am I getting sponge?" mr stinky pants asked.

"yes, in the minute. we just need to go in here first," she answered, leading him toward the bathroom.

"okay," he answered meekly.

ernie paused in the doorway of the kitchen, staring, not really wanting to go in there. dirty plates were piled in the sink. a little table was covered with old jars and tins, packets, cartons, plastic bags everywhere. the floor was littered with rubbish. the smell was awful. worse in here.

he put the cake on the edge of the table. picked it up again after a moment, opened the bag and peeped inside. he could see the sponge, golden and moist, the white filling shining. he licked his lips, staring at it, thinking, what if i took just a little bite? just a bit off the end? mr stinky pants wouldn't notice, would he? just a little bit off the end. mr stinky pants would still get most of it.

ernie took just a little nibble, wrapped the bag around the sponge again, and left the kitchen.

the bathroom door was slightly ajar. he could hear his mother talking to mr stinky pants inside.

"we need to – just let me – oh dear – mr bishop, mr bishop, lean on that and let me – lean on that mr bishop, there, on there, mr bishop, lean on – oh dear…"

ernie stood there not knowing what to do. his stomach rumbled. the last of the sponge disappeared from his mouth with a swirl of his tongue. he glanced from the bathroom door back toward he kitchen.

just one more little nibble, he thought, going back into the kitchen.

he unwrapped the white plastic bag and took a quick bite, wrapped it back up, and left the kitchen again.

there was still lots left for mr stinky pants. lots and lots…

the bathroom door suddenly flew open, propelled by mr stinky pants elbow.

shocked, ernie stared.

"mr bishop!" his mother squealed.

mr stinky pants was leaning forward, one hand on the edge of the bathtub, naked, pale, a brown smear over his white bottom. his mother was standing behind him with a wet flannel, wiping…

"ERNEST!" she yelled, "what are you standing there for? go into the living room. now ernest. what are you staring at? GO INTO THE LIVING ROOM!"

then she kicked the bathroom door closed with her foot.

shaken by the sight, ernie wandered into the dirty living room. what was his mother doing in there? why was she… she was… why would she do that?

he could still hear her.

"…mr bishop, lean on me, lean – mr bishop, mr bishop, lean on me…"

his mother abruptly burst from the bathroom, closed the door after her, flustered.

"go back home ernie. off you go. go back home. i'll be back soon. go home and play with your cars."

"but what about you?"

"i've got to stay awhile and take care of mr bishop."

"why?"

"because there's no one else to do it, that's why ernest."

"how long will you be?"

"not long."

"but i'm hungry."

behind her, mr stinky pants opened the bathroom door and emerged naked like a bony ghost. ernie had never seen a pubic bush before and scowled, staring at his genitals.

mr stinky pants caught sight of ernie and glared furiously. "is that lazy little kaffir still here? has he got the tea yet?"

"go back inside mr bishop. i have to get you some clean clothes."

she shoved him back into the bathroom and closed the door.

a plaintive voice pleaded from behind the door. "am i getting cake?"

"yes. in a minute mr bishop. in a minute." she shook her head, mumbling under her breath, "dear, dear, dear."

"what about me?" ernie asked.

"you go back home and play with your cars ernest. i won't be long."

"am I getting' cake?" mr stinky pants voice asked from behind the moving door handle.

"in a minute mr bishop. in a minute." she turned to ernie. "we have to ask jesus for strength at times like this ernest. we have to pray to jesus to give us strength."

she pointed at the front door. "you go home ernie."

ernie went to the door and paused, glancing back at her in indecision.

"i won't be long," she told him.

ernie went outside.

torrential rain began to pour from the black sky. water dribbled off the balcony. splashing and falling in huge drops and drips. bitter wind lashed his face.

his mother peered at him through a crack in the door. "go straight home ernie. straight home you hear?"

distracted, she turned her head, "oh, mr bishop, mr bishop, oh dear," she sighed in dismay, and closed the door.

ernie shivered as the cold wind buffeted him.

he hoped his mother wouldn't notice he'd eaten some of mr stinky pants sponge. there was lots of it left…

he hurried home, wondering what a kaffir was?

Speedy and
the Shattered man

1. THE SHATTERED MAN.

John Albert Jones extracted his shattered legs from under the rank sheets with a groan, averting his tender eyes from the glowing bedroom curtains.

He retrieved a bottle of his pills from the bedside cabinet; evicting two pills with shaking hands. The yellow capsules stuck to his parched tongue.

Coughing, he retrieved his walking stick from the floor, swaying to his feet, his head pounding.

He hobbled into the bathroom, ran the cold water tap, and scooped a handful of water into his mouth with his cupped hand. Still he struggled to swallow the capsules.

The room span.

He crashed down onto the toilet seat, waiting it out, his hands resting on the top of the curved cane, dipping his head between his elbows.

Beneath the giddiness, the anger simmered, indignant and abrasive.

He couldn't remember the accident.

They'd told him about it afterward…

He'd been crossing the forecourt of the depot for a tea break when a forklift almost ran into him. It managed to swerve in time, but the boxes stacked on it tumbled down on top of him. He'd known the driver too.

He didn't blame Terry at first. It was only afterwards, when he realized he would never recover from the injuries, that he began calling Terry up in the middle of the night to shout drunken abuse at him, or his wife, if she was unlucky enough to answer the phone.

Hell, Terry didn't even lose his job. They'd said that Jones was to blame for the accident; that he had walked out in front of the forklift and Terry wasn't at fault.

The dizziness passed.

Rising unsteadily, he hooked his cane over the rim of the sink and leaned both hands on its edges, catching sight of his reflection. He quickly glanced away. Was that *really* him, that wild man of Borneo staring back from the mirror?

The penny sized nub of soap refused to lather as it twisted and turned vainly in his hands. It broke into crumbs. Buy soap, he told himself, *buy some fuckin' soap!*

It took an age for him to make his way down the stairs, the banister creaking loudly in the quiet house as he clung to it. In the old days he used to run up and down them effortlessly.

He was waiting to hear about a warden controlled bungalow from the council. Then he could sell the house and move.

Huffing and puffing, he reached the bottom of the stairs and sat for a minute, getting his breath back.

Letters sat in an untidy pile underneath the letterbox of the front door. He sat staring at them, panting, vowing to sort through them soon. Had it been weeks since he'd checked them? He lost track of time so easily now. There might be something there about the bungalow.

Grabbing the banister, he groaned as he slowly pulled himself up from the step, and limped into the kitchen.

Dirty plates were stacked in the sink; flies buzzed and crawled above the overstuffed bin; the table was covered with empty cans and bottles. It reeked.

He checked the cupboard for booze; went around the kitchen picking up bottles, shaking cans.

Hobbling back up the hallway, he went into the equally messy living room, checking bottles and cans, without finding a drop. The only thing in one or two of them was his piss.

He slumped dejectedly into the lounge chair, his finger hitting the remote control out of habit more than any wish to watch television.

He flipped through the channels; there was nothing else for it. He would have to go out.

Slipping his old brown duffel coat on over his chequered blue pyjama bottoms and torn green tee shirt, he stuffed some cash into his side pocket, closed the front door on his way out, and shuffled down the street in his slippers.

It was hot.

Perspiration dribbled down his chest and back, his armpits boiling inside the heavy garment. His wheezing, lumbering passage aroused the giggles of two small girls as he passed them in the street, one of them holding her nose.

The door of the shop was propped open. The whiff of warm confectionary hit him as he stepped over the threshold into the dim interior, his eyes adjusting to the light.

Fridges and freezers hummed. A ceiling fan whirred softly overhead, making little impact on the heavy, warm air. The two women behind the counter had been chatting when he walked in but abruptly fell silent.

The alcohol section was next to the till. Grabbing bottles of the cheapest brands of gin and whisky with his free hand, he placed them on the counter.

Neither of the women offered any assistance.

Dressed in light blue pinnies covered in dots, they stood poker faced as the wall of clinking bottles was constructed under their noses. He added a four pack of Special Brew and was done.

He put a steadying hand on the counter, wheezing and swaying, perspiration dripping off his shaggy face.

They weren't two women at all, he realized. One of them was a teenager. The older one he knew; they'd been in school together. They didn't talk now.

Not any more.

With a hostile glare, he fished crumpled notes out of his pocket and dropped them onto the counter. The older woman began swiping the bottles through the till, while the teenager put his goods into carrier bags.

Suddenly giddy, he lost grip on his cane and it toppled to the floor, making a sound like a clap of thunder in the quiet store when it hit the ground. He gripped the counter with both hands, dropping his head.

The teenager hurried out from behind the counter to pick up his cane, bending down at his feet.

Her smile melted into a grimace when she caught the full blast of his neglect.

He snatched the cane off her angrily, one hand clutching the counter, panting. He managed to pocket the change and grabbed the two carrier bags, lurching for the door, eager to return to his corrosive solitude.

2. NOT ANYMORE.

"Is that the one whose wife died?" Ruth, the teenager asked.

Babs glanced out of the window at her stooped, former class mate, jerking awkwardly up the street, bags swinging wildly in one hand, the other jabbing the pavement with the cane.

"That's him."

"What did she die of?"

"Cancer."

"Cancer?"

"Breast cancer."

After a pause, Ruth said, "he must be roasting in that duffel coat."

Babs didn't reply.

"You don't speak anymore, then?"

"No," Babs answered, "not anymore."

"How come?"

Babs thought for a moment, before replying, "he doesn't speak to anyone anymore."

3. SPEEDY.

Speedy heard the clink of bottles and pricked up his ears, spotting Jones across the street.

Who, twisting awkwardly, almost fell, leaning back against a wall.

With the short, quick steps which had earned him his nickname, Speedy darted between two parked cars.

"Wan.Wanna,hand,there,there,boy?"

Jones stared at him helplessly with glassy eyes; a barely perceptible nod was his only reply.

Speedy shifted his tatty grey suit jacket over his arm, grabbed the bags off him, and looked inside.

"Stock.Stockingup,boy?"

Jones just panted and wheezed, nodding again. He tipped his head and managed to lurch off the wall.

Speedy slowly followed him.

"Door's open," Jones mumbled as they reached his gate.

Speedy went in first, pushing the door with his shoulder, holding it open for Jones. The sound of the television made Speedy peer suspiciously into the dim hallway as Jones hobbled past him.

"Who.Who'sthat,boy?"

Jones didn't reply. He tottered into the living room and collapsed into the lounge chair.

"Where.Where'dyou,wannumboy?"

Speedy asked, standing in the doorway.

"Kitchen."

Jones suddenly realized he'd forgotten to buy any food and soap.

"Kit.Kitchen? Where.Where'sthat,boy?"

Jones, exhausted, just tipped his head. Speedy clinked down the hallway.

Speedy paused on the threshold, amazed to see a kitchen that was an even bigger pigsty than his own. He pushed some things to one side and put the bags on the table, dislodging an empty beer can which bounced across the floor with a hollow, metallic clatter.

He darted back up the hallway and peered in at Jones, still wrapped in his duffel coat.

"Sack.Sacked,themaid,boy?"

Jones frowned. "Wha?"

"No.No,offence,boy."

Jones grunted and leaned forward in the chair, trying to drag his arms out of the coat. Speedy darted over, throwing his jacket onto the sofa, and helped him. Jones almost barked to leave him alone, but he needed help and stayed silent. After a minute of wrestling, Speedy stood holding the duffel coat, wondering where to put it.

"Dump it anywhere," Jones told him.

Speedy dropped it behind the sofa.

"What.What,bout,allthat,that,stuff,boy?"

"The beer goes in the fridge. Just leave the rest of it."

Speedy asked hopefully, "Shall.Shall,I,open one,boy?"

"Open a whisky."

Speedy shot back into the kitchen.

He opened the fridge and recoiled from the reek of rotting vegetables. A half-empty bottle of tomato ketchup with a crusty top stood in the milk space. A lettuce and cucumber were in the vegetable drawer, enveloped in white fluffy fungus.

"Fuck.Fuckin'stinks," Speedy mumbled, putting the four pack of Special Brew onto one of the empty shelves and closing the fridge door.

Checking the hallway, making sure Jones wasn't watching, Speedy had a hasty check of the cupboards, searching for food.

He took a shine to a solitary tin of Own Brand baked beans sitting on the top shelf. He licked his lips, knowing he had no food at home, and would be unable to buy any until his giro came the next day. He checked the hallway again, but hesitated about swiping the beans because he had nowhere to hide it. He left it for now, and turned his attention to the whisky.

"Fuck.Fuck's,that?" Speedy exclaimed, kicking something skidding across the floor. It hit the skirting board with a clang. He peered at it. It was a cat food bowl.

"Near.Nearlybroke,my,fuckin',neck.Fuck.Fuckin' moggybowl."

He found two dirty glasses and gave them a perfunctory rinse under the cold tap, then snatched a bottle of whisky from the table and returned to his host, licking his lips in anticipation.

"Near.Nearly,broke,my,fuckin,neck,boy,"

Speedy complained as he entered the living room.

"Hah?"

"That.That,fuckinbo,bowl,onthe,floor,boy."

"Bowl?"

Speedy put the glasses on the already cluttered coffee table.

"Mog.Moggybowl,bowl.What,what's,thatdoin'on the,floor,boy?"

Jones realized he was talking about the cat.

When was the last time he'd seen Flossy? He remembered kicking her when she was whining for food. That was the last he could remember of the cat.

"Where.Where's,themoggy,boy?"

Jones grunted.

"Could.Could'ave,smashed,myhead,headopen,boy."

Jones glared at him.

"Where.Where's,the,moggy,boy?"

"I ate it," Jones told him.

Speedy's face dropped. "You.You,what,boy?"

"You 'eard."

"You.You,bake,it,or,orfry,it,boy?"

Jones grunted again, impatient for some whisky. Speedy was just standing there, clutching it in his hand.

"RS.RSPCA'be,on,to,you,boy,not,not,careful."

"Will they?"

"Fuck.Fuckin,moggies.Foot.Foot,their,arses,I,would, boy."

"Shut up about it," Jones snapped irritably.

"I'm.I'm,on,your,sideboy."

"Don't be."

"Fuck.Fuckin'hate,moggies,me,boy."

"Shut up!"

"All.All,meat,boy,ah?"

"Pour the – "

"Special.Special,fried,moggie,at,the,the, chinkies,boy," Speedy interrupted.

"Nice.Nice,too.Fuck.Fuckin,chinkies."

"Will you shut up and pour some fucking whisky," Jones snapped angrily.

"Sure.Sure,boy."

Speedy twisted the cap off the bottle, poured some golden liquid into the glasses, and put the bottle down. He leaned over and gave a glass to Jones.

"Finally," Jones said gruffly.

Speedy sat down on the tatty sofa and raised his glass. "Cheer.Cheers,boy."

Jones didn't return the toast, guzzling the whisky, draining the glass. He leaned forward, reaching for the bottle.

Speedy jumped up and grabbed it first.

"There.There,you,go,boy," he said, refilling Jones' glass for him. He topped up his own as well, even though he'd hardly touched it.

Jones sat back.

"Any.Any,nibbles,boy?"

Jones stared at Speedy.

If he had any doubts about how far he'd fallen, or been in denial about it before, the sight of Speedy in his home, in his living room, hit it home for him.

In the old days, when his wife was still alive, before the accident, it would have been unthinkable.

Jones quickly shifted his thoughts away from Ann. He didn't want to dwell on her.

Nausea churned in his middle. As numb as he was,

Speedy being there sparked profound shame in him. He realized that he had become on par with Speedy. People out there in the town regarded them both as outcasts, as misfits. People shunned them both.

"Any.Any,nibblesboy?"

Jones could remember Speedy from school.

Speedy had been in the 'special' class. Along with an autistic boy who picked at bleeding scabs on his face, a girl who looked like a plucked, startled turkey, and a boy who always had a nappy poking up from the top of his trousers.

"Any.Any,food,boy?"

Jones recalled Speedy lurking in some solitary part of the playground, pacing nervously like a cornered animal, trying to avoid the girls who taunted him, and the boys who bullied him. On occasion surrounded by a group and dragged off for some hidden humiliation.

Yet when Jones pictured Speedy back then, in school, he saw him as he was seeing him now. Balding, greasy, wild hair, face bristling with white stubble, his gut pushing out of the soiled white shirt hanging over the belt of his second hand suit. He couldn't picture Speedy as a boy, or a teenager; couldn't remember him looking any younger than he was now.

Maybe it was the accident stealing pieces of his memory.

"Fuck.Fuckin'starvin',boy."

Jones took a drink.

And now here Speedy was, in his living room, after all these years, drinking his whisky.

How could such a thing have happened?

Speedy looked at Jones, but his host was ignoring him. He took his tin out of his pocket and began making a roll up with expert, yellowed fingers. After he'd finished, he returned his rizzlas and tobacco to the tin, shoved it back into his shirt pocket, and planted his limp creation into his mouth.

"Any.Any,nibbles,boy?"

"No," Jones snapped.

Speedy stared at Jones blankly for a moment, and then lit his roll up.

Jones switched channels, settling on an old western with a skinny John Wayne sauntering around under a huge white cowboy hat.

"Black.Black,andwhite,boy," Speedy complained.

Jones sipped his drink. He was feeling a little better now. The alcohol was working.

"Black.Black,andwhite,boy,"

Speedy repeated in agitation.

"I'm not blind."

"No.No,offence,boy."

Jones drained his glass. From the corner of his eye he noticed Speedy quickly grab his glass and knock back its contents. As Jones leaned forward, Speedy did too, holding out his glass.

"Fuck.Fuckin'goodstuff,that,boy."

Jones filled both their glasses with a sigh, and sat back. Clouds of pungent smoke began to curl from Speedy's seat.

"Ee's.Ee's,ah,fuckinpuffta,boy."

"Who?"

"John.John,fuckin',Wayne,boy."

"A puffta? Since when?"

"Tell.Tellin'you,boy."

"First I've heard of it."

"Tell.Tellin'you,boy.Well,well,known,that,boy."

"By who?"

"Me.Me,boy."

"And who else?"

"Every.Everyone,boy."

Jones noticed one of his toes had dried blood on it; the toenails poking through his dirty, shredded socks badly needed trimming; they were starting to resemble talons.

"Fuck.Fuckin'tranny'eewas,boy."

"Huh?"

"Fuck.Fuckin'transvestite,boy."

Jones laughed. It was the first time he'd laughed in ages. "John Wayne?"

"Tell.Tellin'you,boy."

"Right."

"Used.Used,to,wear,a,fuckin'dressboy.Pan.Panties. Stock.Stockins'The.The,lot."

"Sure."

"Tell.Tellin'you,boy."

Jones smiled. Christ, was he actually enjoying Speedy's company? What the hell was going on?

Speedy suddenly pointed his hand at the television, a tendril of smoke twisting up from his roll up, and imitated a gun. "Pow.Pow.Powpowpow…"

Jones scowled.

"Pow.Pow,powpowpowpowpow…"

"Who are you, Billy the Kid?" Jones asked.

"Fuck.Fuckin'right,boy.Pow.Pow,powpowpow…"

Jones suddenly thought about Flossy.

The grey patterns on her fur; how she used to snuggle up on his lap. He missed her. What the hell had happened to her? He felt hysteria welling up, and almost sobbed. Quickly, he forced it back down into the dank pit festering in his gut. He took a drink; looked at Speedy.

"Pow.Pow.Powpowpowpow…" Speedy, getting carried away, used his other hand to imitate fanning the hammer of his imaginary pistol; whiskey jumped over the side of the glass, dotting his lap. "Fuck.Fuckin'ell." He quickly glanced pop-eyed from his lap to Jones, as if expecting a reprimand. "All.All'is fuck,fuckin'fault,boy," he said, blaming John Wayne. "Ee.Ee'fuckin'started,it."

Jones, wanting to feel wasted, took another drink.

"Stead.Steady,on.Not.Not,fuckinchristmas,boy."

Speedy guzzled his whisky and went for the bottle. Jones held his glass out. After Speedy refilled both their glasses, he resumed his shoot out with John Wayne.

"Pow.Pow.Powpowpowpowpow…"

Onscreen, a cowboy tumbled through flying glass from a first floor window into the street, dead.

Speedy whooped.

"Got.Got'im.See.See,that,boy." Speedy blew on the end of his finger, as if blowing on the end of a pistol. He pointed his hand at Jones and shot him. "Pow.Pow.Powpowpowpowpow…"

It began to grate on Jones. Speedy giggled. He pointed the pistol back at the screen. "Fuck.Fuckin'arse,

Bandit.Pow.Pow.Powpowpowpow…"

"I think you got him," Jones said tactfully, hoping to shut him up.

"Ee.Ee'sfuckin,goodshot,though,JohnWayne,boy."

"Well, he's had enough practice."

Speedy sat back, sipping his drink. He sucked the last

life out of the roll up and leaned forward, dropping it into the spout of one of the empty bottles on the coffee table. It sizzled a second in the bottom.

Speedy sat forward, twisting his head back and for as if searching for something.

"Des.Desperate,for,a,piss,boy."

"What?"

"Need.Needto,piss,boy."

"Go piss then."

Speedy peered at Jones.

Jones realized that Speedy was wondering whether or not Jones was going to let him use the toilet in the house.

"Upstairs," Jones told him.

"The.The,bogup,upstairs,boy?"

Jones nodded.

"Can.Can,I,trust,you,boy?"

"Huh?"

"Don't.Don't,drink,it,all,"

Speedy cackled, "Will.Will,you,boy."

Jones glanced at the bottle of whisky, frowning.

"O.Only,jokin'boy."

Speedy hurried past and went out of the door.

4. LIBERTY.

Giddy with liberation, Speedy climbed the stairs.

No one had ever let him wander around their house before. No one had ever let him use their bathroom before.

He reached the top of the stairs, eyes darting eagerly from door to door along the landing.

He went into the bathroom, took a piss, and deliberately didn't flush.

He emerged back onto the landing, and had a quick look over the banister to make sure his host wasn't watching him. The sound of gunshots and shouting boomed up the walls.

He crossed to one of the doors and opened it, peering inside. It was the master bedroom. The bed was unmade; the curtains closed. He went in, stepping over detritus and clothes littering the carpet.

Sliding open a drawer, his fingers searched but found nothing interesting. He tried another, and another. His breathing quickened when he discovered a neat pile of women's panties. He picked up a pair and sniffed them, his hand diving into his pocket and squeezing his cock. He sniffed them all, one at a time, rubbing them across the stubble of his face. He put them all carefully back, but kept a silky, lacy black G-string, shoving it into his trouser pocket as a keepsake.

The intense tang of warm leather enveloped him as he opened the wardrobe. There were belts hanging from a rail, shoes and boots lined up along the base. The shirts and jackets hanging on coat hangers didn't interest him.

He went back out onto the landing. There were more doors, more rooms. He took a peek over the banister, half expecting to see Jones staring up at him angrily, but there was only the sound of galloping horses.

Speedy crept into a box room. It was bare except for a ripped poster of Spiderman on the wall. He spotted something in the corner, and bent down to retrieve it. It was a shattered picture frame, with a photograph still inside – a family portrait; a smiling couple with a small, smiling boy sat between them, all dressed in their Sunday best. It took a moment for Speedy to realize that the clean, grinning, immaculately attired man in the photograph was his host downstairs.

Speedy heard him coming up the stairs.

In a panic, he dropped the frame and hurried onto the landing, peeking over the banister.

No one was there.

Relieved, he took a final glance along the landing, and was about to go back downstairs when he remembered he hadn't flushed the toilet. He quickly went into the bathroom and did it, hoping his ruse would disguise his prying.

5. UNCARING.

Pipes rattled in the walls.

Jones, who knew every creak and groan of his house, knew exactly what Speedy was up to.

What surprised him was how little he cared.

He heard Speedy coming down the stairs.

"Find what you wanted?" Jones asked when he entered.

"Found.Found,the,bog,boy."

"You're flying low."

"Buh.Boy?"

Jones tipped his head at Speedy's crotch. Speedy looked down at his gaping fly.

"You.You,after,mycock,boy?"

Jones scowled at him angrily.

Speedy zipped up. "O.Only,joking,boy."

Speedy sat down, reached for the whisky bottle, and refilled his glass. It irked Jones the way he sat back with such a self satisfied air. He looked so damn at home.

"This.This,queer,stillon,boy?" Speedy asked, staring at the television.

"Looks like it."

"Bald.Bald'eewas,boy.Bald.Bald,as,a,badgers,

arse.Wore.Wore,a,wig,boy."

Speedy guzzled his drink, his lips wet.

"Where.Where's,the,injuns,boy?I,I,likeinjuns."

"'Avin a curry."

"Buff.Buffalo,curry,boy," Speedy cackled.

Jones reached for the whisky.

"Fuck.Fuckin'savages,boy.Cut,cutyour,ballsoff,they,would,boy."

"Would they?"

Speedy drained his glass and set it down, smacking his lips together, then reached into his pocket for his tin.

"When.When,they,gonna,kill'im,boy?"

"The Duke never gets killed; don't you know that."

Speedy glanced at him, bewildered by the remark, before dropping his head; swiftly, he made himself another roll up before tucking his kit back into his pocket.

"Fast.Fastest,faggot,in,thewest,boy."

Smoke began curling across the room. They sat in silence for a time. The film finished, and Jones watched the rolling obituaries on the screen.

"Any.Anythin'else,on,boy?"

Jones tossed the remote into Speedy's lap. "Help yourself."

Ecstatic, Speedy picked it up and began flipping through the channels.

"Love.LoveColumbo,me.Is.IsColumbo,on,boy?"

He continued flipping through the channels.

"Fuck.Fuck,all,on,boy."

The doorbell rang.

Speedy stopped, his head swivelling, his eyes darting from side to side nervously.

"Who.Who,the,fuck's'that,boy?"

"How should I know?"

The doorbell chimed again.

"Who.Who,the,fuck's,that,boy?"

"I don't know."

"Fuck.Fuckin'Jehovahs,probably,boy.Fuck.Fuckin'cunts them,Jehovahs,boy."

Jones didn't budge.

"Not.Not,answering,boy?"

Jones ignored him. The doorbell chimed again.

Speedy jumped up and dashed to the window, peering through a crack in the curtain.

"Fuck.Fuckin'kid,boy."

Jones forehead creased up; he knew who it was. He hoped he would just go away.

But the doorbell rang again.

"Want.Want,me,to,to,tell,'imto,'opp,it,boy?"

"No," Jones snapped angrily, "just mind your own business."

"No.No,offence,boy."

Speedy peeked through the curtains again, glancing at Jones meekly, as if expecting another telling off.

The doorbell went again.

Speedy glanced at Jones, opened his mouth to say something, but changed his mind and peeked through the curtains again.

"Will you get away from the fuckin' window," Jones barked at him.

Speedy jerked back as if someone had yanked him.

"No.No,offence,boy."

Jones leaned forward, beginning the arduous task that

standing up had become for him now. He grasped his cane and began shakily to rise. Speedy hurried to his side and put a hand on his elbow.

"Did I ask for your help?" Jones snarled at him.

Speedy recoiled. "No.No,offence,boy."

Jones slumped back into the chair dizzily, his head hanging forward. Speedy didn't dare offer any further help. Jones struggled to his feet while Speedy sat back down and sipped his whisky.

He watched Jones wobble across the room and vanish out of the door.

Speedy immediately jumped up, peeping around the doorway; Jones was jerking his way slowly toward the front door.

Speedy shot into the kitchen.

He quickly opened the cupboard and snatched the tin of Own Brand baked beans from the shelf. He paused in the kitchen doorway, checking on Jones, who had almost reached the front door.

Speedy darted back into the living room. He put the tin of beans in the side pocket of his jacket and sat down, more than pleased with himself.

Now he could eat later.

Grinning, he poured himself another drink and picked up the remote control.

6. TIM.

Tim stepped into the living room, startled when his eyes met Speedy's.

Speedy recognised the boy from the shattered picture he'd found upstairs.

"Where you gone?" Jones asked gruffly from the hallway.

Bewildered, the boy backed out of the room as Speedy fixed his beady eyes on him.

Tim almost bumped into Jones reversing back into the hall.

"The kitchen!" Jones barked at him.

Shuffling into the living room, he gave Speedy an order. "Time to leave."

Speedy sat up, eyes popping. "What.What's,up,boy?"

"You're leaving, *that's* what's up."

"Who.Who's,that,kid,boy?"

"My son."

"Your.Yourson?"

"That's right."

Jones stood waiting. Speedy didn't move, staring at Jones blankly, the remote control hanging from one hand and the glass of whisky clutched in the other.

"Come on," Jones prompted him.

"Now.Now,boy?"

"No time like the present."

"Some.Somethin'wrong,boy?"

"Come on," Jones growled.

Speedy knocked his whisky back and clacked the empty glass onto the coffee table. He stared at the whisky bottle longingly. "One.One,more,boy?"

Jones shook his head.

"Quick.Quick,one,boy?"

"Do I have to throw you out?"

"O.Only,jokin'boy."

Speedy stood up, picking up his jacket, feeling the weight of the tin of beans hanging down in the pocket.

"You got something poking out there," Jones told him.

Speedy flushed, thinking his theft had been spotted, but when he looked down it was the panties, his *other* theft, hanging from his pocket that Jones was referring to. Speedy quickly shoved them deep into his pocket, glancing at Jones, wondering if he realized what they were. But a bleary eyed Jones seemed distracted, leaning exhausted onto his cane, swaying.

"Let yourself out," he murmured.

"See.See,you,then,boy," Speedy answered, hugging his jacket to his chest, darting through the door, down the hallway, and out of the front door.

Jones went into the kitchen. His son was standing in the midst of the domestic chaos, gazing at the mess.

"What was *he* doing here?" Tim asked, looking at his Dad questioningly.

"Never mind him. What are *you* doin' here?" Jones

asked angrily, wheezing.

Tim stared at him, hurt. "I've come to see you."

"Why?"

Tim said nothing.

"Why aren't you at School?"

"It's the holidays."

"Is it?"

"When can I come home, Dad?" Tim asked suddenly.

"Home?" Jones trembled. Oh Christ! What sort of home could he offer him now? "You live with your auntie now."

"I want to come back and live with you though, Dad."

"I'm *not* your Dad anymore," Jones snapped spitefully. "You went to live with *them*."

"Only cos you told me to."

"When I got all smashed up."

"I didn't want to go and live with them."

"Just because I got all smashed up, you went off with them."

"I didn't."

"Didn't want me then," Jones muttered in self pity.

"What?"

"You went off with them."

"I didn't."

Jones couldn't think straight. He just wanted to sit down. "You DID!" he bellowed.

Tim shuddered as if he'd been hit. "You told me. You told me it'd only be for awhile."

The booze was messing with Jones' brain. Maybe he did tell him to go. Maybe he did. What did it matter now anyway?

"So you went," Jones said weakly.

"Only because -"

"You didn't need your Dad anymore."

"But I do."

"Your Dad's no good to anyone anymore."

"I only went because you told me I *had* to."

"I never."

"But you did," Tim protested.

"Why would I do that?"

"You said, you said, it would be best."

"Best for who?"

"I dunno. That's what you said."

The whisky said different. He couldn't remember, didn't want to remember. Why would he say that?

Jones was too damn bitter to love anymore.

"Dad?"

"Go home," Jones snapped.

"But this is home."

"Not anymore. Your home is with your auntie."

The truth was – Jones just didn't want him around. Tim reminded him of his wife and the life they'd had before everything imploded. Tim reminded him of everything he'd lost and would never get back. Of how broken he was not just in body but in spirit. He hadn't felt like a parent for some considerable time. Tim was like an alien to him now; some strange creature from a far away land.

How could he possibly move back? Look at the place.

"But I want to move back here," Tim protested again.

"Oh don't be silly Tim," Jones answered in exasperation, "you can't move back her."

"But why?"

Jones trembled with rage.

Oh Jesus, what did Tim want him to say? Did he want him to admit the truth? That he just wasn't capable of looking after him anymore? He couldn't even look after himself, for god's sake. And if he got the bungalow the house would be gone anyway.

"Can't you see Tim?" Jones croaked.

Tim began to whimper. Jones felt the floor shift under his feet. He lurched out of the door, up the hallway, and returned to the living room. He collapsed into the chair, staring glassy eyed at the television. As numb as he was, he still felt too much. He reached for the whisky bottle. From the corner of his eye, he could see Tim watching him from the doorway.

"Are you still here?" he grumbled, pouring himself a drink.

Tim stared at him, searching desperately for his real Dad under that shaggy, pungent, angry man.

"Dad?"

The word cut into Jones' like a dagger.

"Dad?"

A ball of phlegm caught in Jones' throat. He spluttered.

"Dad?"

"Christ!"

"Dad?"

Hissing, "stop it."

Tim had moved closer now, standing beside the chair arm.

"Dad?"

"Stop."

"Dad?"

"Get out."

"Dad?"

"GET OUT TIM!"

Tim began to cry, his chin dipping into his chest.

Jones' voice swelled with rage. "*GET OUT TIM!*"

Tim turned and ran. Jones heard the back door slam and sat there watching meat and onions sizzle in a frying pan.

The isolation was suddenly absolute.

He threw the remote control across the room and began to weep.

7. IN THE WOODS.

Tim ran blindly.

His father didn't want him; it struck him like a punch that his Dad didn't exist anymore.

He cleared the lanes, the streets, and plunged into open fields, until he collapsed in a sea of wild grass, panting.

As he lay there, staring up at the swaying, towering stalks, the soft rustle of the field calmed him. Jumbled pictures of his father raced through his mind. His father and his mother, back before his mother became ill, before his father had the accident.

His torment gradually subsided as he watched the bowing green stalks and boundless blue sky.

Suddenly, he heard something.

Listening, he held his breath.

Someone was thrashing through the grass, and stopped only feet way.

Tim tensed up, waiting.

Finally, whoever it was set off again. He heard the thrashing dwindle into the distance, relaxed, and drifted off into sleep.

He dreamt his Dad was floating around his house on a flying carpet, sitting on it cross legged like the Mekon in his

Dan Dare comic.

Abruptly, he awoke, and sat up, rubbing his eyes, wondering what time it was.

Standing up, his head cleared the grass and he scanned the surrounding field. There was no one around, only the gentle undulation of the wild grass and a single, white fluffy cloud sailing past in the blue summer sky.

He walked to the bottom of the field and entered a wood via a dirt trail leading up into the trees.

It was shaded and cool inside. The odd shaft of sunlight pierced through the shadows. He followed the narrow, mud path deep into the thick of it, and sat down for a rest, against a huge, gnarled old tree. Above him, in the dense, leafy branches, birds were singing. He listened until there was a distinct snap from somewhere close by and the feathered chorus abruptly stopped its reverie.

Tim was shocked to see Speedy suddenly come ambling up the path toward him with his quick, jerky steps, grey jacket draped over his arm, eyes locked onto Tim's.

Speedy darted closer, dark stains under his armpits, never taking his eyes off Tim.

"All.Alright,boy?"

As Speedy drew near, Tim stood up, feeling the bumpy trunk sliding against his back.

"All.Alrightboy?" Speedy asked again, wiping his forearm across his glistening forehead.

Tim remembered the person he'd heard earlier thrashing through the grass.

"Fuck.Fuckin'ot,boy."

Speedy was close now. Tim tensed, ready to bolt.

"Your.Your,father,know,where,you,areboy?"

Mention of his father made Tim hesitate.

"Cat.Catgot,your,tongue,boy?"

Tim shook his head mechanically. Speedy was so close now, he could smell stale cigarettes, B.O., and whisky.

Speedy's hand suddenly shot out and grabbed Tim's arm. "It.It'salright,boy."

Tim yelped and struggled.

"I.I,won't,tell,boy."

Tim felt the grip tighten painfully around his arm.

"Keep.Keep,a,secretme,boy."

Cold fear twisted in Tim's belly when he saw the look on Speedy's face.

"Can.Canyou,keep,a,secret,boy?"

"Let go," Tim shrieked, trying to yank his arm from the iron grip.

"A.A,now," Speedy cautioned.

"LET GO!" Tim yelled.

"Now.Now,boy."

Tim flailed around, trying to free himself. Speedy gripped him tightly with both hands.

"Now.Now,boy."

"LET GO!"

"Easy.Easynow."

"LET – "

"A.A,now."

Tim stopped struggling, panting.

"That.That'sbetter,boy."

When Tim felt the fierce grip slacken, he dropped his shoulder and deftly twisted free, the same manoeuvre he'd used dozens of times when wrestling with his friends.

"Oy.Oy," Speedy yelled, making another grab for him.

But Tim bounded away.

Speedy dropped his jacket, got his feet tangled up in the sleeves, stumbling.

"Fuck.Fuckin'cunt," he shrieked.

Tim ran into the bushes opposite the path, but immediately realized he'd made a mistake. They were too dense. He tried to back out but Speedy was there.

"You.You,little,cunt."

Speedy yanked Tim violently, throwing him to the ground; losing his balance and falling on top of him. As they scrabbled around on the ground, Tim's trainer came out of the dust and slammed into Speedy's face, making his ears ring and his eyes water.

Tim jumped to his feet, frantically glancing back.

Speedy couldn't believe the boy was escaping again; he noticed something glint in the dirt near his hand.

The tin of beans he'd stolen from Jones kitchen.

Speedy grabbed it and reared up, throwing it desperately at the fleeing boy.

The can bounced off Tim's head and Tim fell.

"Fuck.Fuckin'teach,ya."

Speedy spat, blood and mud in his mouth, the little shit, and regained his feet.

Tim was whimpering, peering back at Speedy with horrified eyes.

Speedy dropped heavily onto Tim, pinning him to the ground with his knees; he could see blood on the back of Tim's head.

"Fuck.Fuckinlittle,shit."

On his stomach, Tim screeched. The sound shattered something inside Speedy.

"Shut.Shuttup."

Tim kept screeching.

"Shut.Shutthe,fuck,shut,shut."

Screeching.

"Pack.Packit,in."

Screeching at the top of his lungs.

Speedy began to panic. What if someone heard? What if someone came?

Speedy pushed the back of Tim's head hard into the dirt. He slipped his hand around and clamped it over Tim's mouth, but Tim bit into it, making Speedy yelp in pain. He yanked his hand away, looking at the bite mark imprinted there.

"Little.Littlefuckin'shit!"

Tim began screeching again. Speedy punched him in the back. Tim stopped for a moment, but then screeched even louder, cutting Speedy's nerves to the quick.

"SHUT.SHUTUP."

Tim kept screeching. From the corner of his eye, Speedy saw the can. He snatched it up and started hitting him over the head with it until Tim went limp.

He stopped, drenched in sweat. The tin was covered in blood and hair. He dropped it and looked at his bloody, shaking hands.

Getting up, he glanced down at Tim to make sure he wasn't moving; nervously scanning the woods to reassure himself no one was there. He looked at his bloody hands again. A terror coiled in his belly and he retched, ejecting the whisky he'd drunk earlier.

The blood felt repulsive; warm and sticky on his hands. He bent down and wiped them on the kid's tee-shirt.

Tim had an expression of pained astonishment on his

bloody, mud streaked face.

Speedy stepped away from the body, staring at it with incomprehension. The boy's eyes were wide open and staring up at him.

He glanced around the woods again. No one saw, he told himself. No one saw anything. Just get away. Get away quickly. Go now.

...*now,now*...

He picked up his jacket and the bloody, dented tin of beans, wiping it as best he could on the kid's tee shirt.

Darting down the trail, he left the woods as fast as he could.

8. HOME.

Speedy went straight home, not glancing at a soul on the way, especially not the pack of teenage boys who shouted sarcastic abuse at him; guiltily thinking people were staring at him; that people somehow knew what he'd done. His anxiety shifted into relief when he breathlessly stepped inside his flat and closed the door behind him.

Immediately, he went to the front window and peered beyond the torn, yellowed net curtain, just to check no one had followed him.

There was a solitary boy passing, clattering a can noisily along the pavement with the toe of his trainer.

He quickly pulled the curtains closed, even though it was still light. The silence inside seemed ominous, and spooked him. He could hear the can clattering outside in the street. He switched on the television and anxiously sat. After awhile he calmed down and what happened in the woods began to fade from his mind. The television soothed him. He flipped from channel to channel, not watching anything for more than a minute or so, wishing he'd swiped some booze from Jones' place before he'd left. That's what he needed, something to take the edge off.

And he was starving.

Gingerly, he took the tin of beans from his muddy jacket pocket and went into the kitchen. The dented can was bloody. Pushing the memory of why from his mind, he held the can under the tap, letting water pour over it. He peeled off the bloody, torn label and put the silver tin on the draining board, gleaming now. The soggy paper from the label collected in the plug hole alongside long, alien black hairs.

"Fuck.Fuckin'starvin," he mumbled.

He stabbed the tin with an opener and worked it around as far as he could, easing the sharp, jagged lid up carefully.

He shook the beans into a battered saucepan, ran tap water into the can, swished it around, and poured the juice onto the beans.

"Fuck.Fuckin'starvin."

He crushed the tin in his hand and threw it into the overflowing bin. A black, buzzing mass reared up at the disturbance.

"Fuck.Fuckers," he cursed, waving his hand around as they buzzed around his head.

What little bread he had was mouldy, so he cut the green bits off and put what was left of the stiff slices under the grill. Then he slid the obese black bin bag from the plastic bin and tied it up.

"Fuck.Fuckers," he cursed as the flies cavorted around him.

Opening the back door, he ferried the bin outside. When he returned, the pleasing aroma of beans sweetened the air, and he involuntarily smacked his lips together, his stomach rumbling. "Fuck.Fuckin'starvin."

Standing over the saucepan, he stared down into the

bubbling beans longingly, stirring them with a small metal teaspoon. His yearning stomach gargled. He checked the toast, turned it over, and stirred the beans again, ignoring the lingering flies. When the toast was brown, he dropped it onto a plate, picked up the saucepan, and poured the steaming beans on top.

They tasted like nothing he'd ever eaten. There was bean juice all over his beard when he'd finished. He made himself a mug of black, sweet tea and sat in front of the television; belching his judgement on a game show contestant.

"Fuck.Fuckin'brainlesscunt."

He watched television late into the night, then went to bed.

Drifting to sleep, he was ushered into his mother's room in the hospice, the nurse marooning him there to pay his final respects. He waited an age before stepping closer, approaching the bed nervously, staring at that thing on the bed they said was his mother; oversized white dentures jutting from a wasted, unknown face in an obscene smile that unnerved him.

Then he was back in the woods, battering the boy's head with his makeshift weapon.

As he stood up, the bloody can dripping in his hand, he noticed someone watching him from the shadows under the trees. He jolted in panic. His terror turned to ice cold shame when he realized the person watching him was in fact his mother, shaking her head in dismay and disgust.

liss.listenmum... he tried to explain, make her understand what had happened. *liss.listen,mum...*

He jerked awake on his bed, staring into the darkness.

His mother was standing at the foot of the bed, shaking her head at him disapprovingly. He saw the shame clouding her face.

liss.listenmum...

She slowly turned and moved away. He wanted to call her back, but his voice dried up. She returned quickly, holding a dog lead; the lead hung down into blackness, and he couldn't see what was attached to the other end of it. His mother glanced down at whatever it was and twitched on the lead, nodding at her son. He heard something stir. His mother, after glancing at him with angry, accusing eyes, bent down into the blackness and unhooked the lead. Then he felt the jolt of betrayal. The boy came writhing up from the darkness, crawling up over the bottom of his bed. Speedy glanced at his mother and saw her stern, set face; realizing she was against him now, just like everyone else. The boy twisted his way up onto the bed, bloody slime trailing after him, his face a destroyed mess, snarling at him through smashed teeth like a wild animal. The obscenity crawled up his legs. He glanced at his mother imploringly, but she turned away.

liss.listenmum...

Speedy woke up, sweating and whimpering, blinking into the blackness, until he realized there was nothing there. That it was a dream.

That he'd pissed himself.

Outside, it was dark, quiet.

Disorientated, he got up and turned on the lights, scanning the room, still half expecting someone to be there, watching him. But it was empty. There was a wet patch on the bed. He peeled off his soaking underwear, cursing, and pulled the sheet off the mattress, put them in the bathtub, and drowned them in running water. While they floated he went into the living room, sat down, and turned on the television, wishing he had a drink. If only he had a drink.

He made himself a roll up and smoked. After awhile he drooped and nodded off.

9. POST OFFICE.

Speedy jerked awake, his head pounding, his mouth sore.
what.Whatwas,that?
He heard a metallic thump outside the curtains. After a tense moment, he relaxed; it was only the bin collection.

Padding to the window, he peeked out through the closed curtains and saw men in yellow plastic tank tops tossing black bin bags into a yawning refuse lorry. One of them passed his window dragging Speedy's bin behind him. Speedy shrank back, letting the curtain drop into place, dimly thinking, in back of his mind, that the empty tin of beans he'd thrown in the bin last night was being taken away.

He sat back in the chair.

A red and inflamed bite mark throbbed on his hand; the sight of it sent a spasm of unease through him.

He went into the kitchen and made a cup of strong black tea.

His tobacco was long gone when his giro finally clattered through the letterbox.

He dressed and went out, clutching the giro like a life belt.
It was crowded in the post office.

Hot.

A short, spindly old man wearing a white string vest sat pressing on a walking stick, scowling at Speedy as he entered.

Speedy ignored him and joined the queue.

His odour was immediately noticed. The immaculately dressed old woman in front of him glanced back at him sharply, wrinkling her nose, and shuffled forward. A young mother with a pushchair had two kids who were scampering around. They ignored her hissed admonishment to pack it in.

Speedy began to shake. He didn't like it; it was too crowded in there. Sweat began pouring off him. They were all watching him. The kids paused in their play and stared at him open mouthed.

But he couldn't return later. He needed his money *now*. Staring down the queue, crushing the giro in his hand, he wondered what was taking so long.

The old bastard in the vest wouldn't stop glaring at him.

Speedy swiped his arm across his dribbling forehead.

Finally, it was his turn.

He pushed the crumpled giro under the window. The tubby young woman behind the counter grinned at him from behind thick glasses.

"Mornin'. How are you?"

Speedy, not listening, stared at her hands.

"You well?"

He looked up. "Huh.Huh?"

"In yourself, I mean?"

"My.Myself,girl?"

He glanced to the side and saw the old man was still watching him.

"Ole.Olefuckin'cunt," Speedy hissed, loud enough for the teller to hear. Frowning, she pulled back, and quickly counted out his money and slid it through the metal hollow under the window into his eager hands.

"Next," she snapped, hostile now.

'fat.Fatfoureyedcunt,' Speedy thought as he turned away clutching his money.

Elated, he left the post office and went immediately to the local shop. He walked out again with a bulging carrier bag and took it home.

In his kitchen, he unpacked beer, gin, margarine, baked beans, bread and tobacco. He made himself beans on toast, and after eating, put the dirty dishes in the sink. He sat, drank some gin, and smoked, feeling like a king.

Until that terrible gnawing in his stomach began again.

Before he knew it, he was leaving the flat, stepping outside into the sunshine, and found himself knocking on Jones door.

When no one answered, he knocked again. After waiting, he tapped timidly on the window. Finally Jones opened the door, scowling at him.

"It's you," he growled unhappily.

"All.Alright,boy?"

Speedy thought he was going to be angrily dismissed, but something inside Jones seemed to capitulate. He flicked his head at Speedy in invitation and retreated back inside the gloomy house, lurching slowly up the hallway on his walking stick. Speedy trailed him into the living room. The television was on. Jones sat on the chair, Speedy on the sofa.

"To what do I owe this pleasure?" Jones asked sarcastically.

"Thought.Thought,I'd,popround,boy."

"Lucky me."

"Black.Black,andwhite'gain,boy?"

"What happened to your face?" Jones asked, noticing the swelling around Speedy's mouth.

Speedy quickly touched it, remembering the kid kicking him.

"Nuth.Nothin'boy."

There was a bottle of whisky on the go, sitting uncapped on the coffee table. Jones noticed Speedy look at it and lick his lips.

"Help yourself," he murmured.

"Cheer.Cheers,boy."

The glass from the day before sat where Speedy had left it. He filled it.

"Who.Who'sthat,boy?"

"Alan Ladd."

Speedy chuckled, "Fuck.Fuckin'midget,boy

"Not quite."

"Fuck.Fuckin'shortarse,boy."

"He was."

Speedy smugly sat back, sipping his whisky. He took out his tobacco and made himself a roll up. Pungent smoke was soon floating across the room.

"Short.Shortarse."

Jones said nothing.

"I.I,like,Columbo,boy."

"Do you."

"I.I,like,Columbo,me,boy," he repeated.

Speedy watched a stocky man throwing a fit onscreen.

"Who.Who'sthat,boy?"

"William Bendix."

"What.What's,itcalled,boy?"

"The Blue Dahlia."

"Old.Older,than,a,grannies,snatch,thisboy."

Jones had a splitting headache.

"'E.Ee,used,to,standon,on,a,box,boy."

Jones grunted.

"Know.Know,that,boy?"

"Did he?"

"Fuck.Fuckin'right,boy."

"Huh."

"Fuck.Fuckin'midget,boy."

Speedy fell silent. He finished his drink, leaned forward, picked up the whisky bottle, and re-filled his glass uninvited. Jones noticed, was annoyed, but said nothing.

"Fuck.Fuckin'nutter," Speedy commented when Bendix threw another fit.

"This.This,film'sallnutters,nutters,andmidgets,boy."

Jones pounding head grew worse.

"I'd.I'dfoot,that,fuck,fuckin'midgetupthe,arse,boy."

"WILL YOU SHUT UP," Jones shouted at him.

Speedy froze, peering at him.

"Just.Just,sayin'boy," he mumbled.

"Just watch it, will you."

"I.Iam,boy." After a short pause. "Black.Blackand whiteboy."

Speedy took a final suck on his roll up and dropped it into one of the empty bottles. He quickly made another. Fresh smoke began crowding the air.

"Col.Columbo,I,like,boy."

Jones shot him an evil look.

"You.You,like,Columbo,boy?"

"I'm watching this," Jones told him quietly.

"No.No,offence,boy."

Next time Speedy knocked on his door, Jones decided, he wouldn't answer.

"When.When'sColumbo,on,boy?"

"I don't fuckin' know."

"No.No,offence,boy."

Speedy fell silent. He drank, filled his glass, and drank some more, free and easy with Jones' booze.

Suddenly he asked, "Where.Where's,thekid,boy?"

"Hah?"

"The.The,kid,boy?"

"What kid?"

"The.The,kid.From.From,yesterday,boy?"

"Huh? Oh, you mean Tim?"

"The.Thekid,boy."

Jones gave him questioning look. Speedy dropped his eyes.

"You mean Tim?" Jones asked again.

"Just.Just,wondered,boy."

"He doesn't live here," Jones answered, adding a moment later, "anymore."

"Just.Just,wondered,boy."

Jones questioning gaze lingered on Speedy a moment longer, then he re-focused on Alan Ladd.

"No.No,offence,boy."

They sat in silence.

Then, "fuck.Fuckin'midget,boy."

Jones growled loudly in exasperation and dropped his finger on the remote control, switching channels. He flipped from channel to channel angrily. "No. No. No Columbo. No Columbo. Satisfied?"

A darkened, glossy game show studio replaced 'The Blue Dahlia'.

"No.No,offence,boy."

Jones sighed, scowling at the screen. Make the most of it, he thought, this'll be the last time.

"I.I,should,go,on on,one,of,these,boy.Make. Make,a,fortune,

I,would,boy."

Jones grunted sceptically.

"Name the capital of Bangladesh?" someone was asked onscreen.

"Easy.Easy,boy.Kalalumpty."

"Dhaka it is. Take another or pass?"

"Fuck.Fuckin'ell."

"Who did the then Cassius Clay defeat to become the heavyweight boxing champion of the world?"

"Joe.JoeFrazier," Speedy whooped.

The contestant thought about it.

"Ease.Easy.Joe.JoeFrazier."

"Sonny Liston is correct. Take another or pass?"

"Fuck.Fuckin'ell.Get.Get'em,all,usually,boy."

"Sure you do."

"Do.Do,boy."

"Do,do,do be do," Jones crooned mockingly.

"Fuck.Fuckin'right,boy."

"Name the biblical strongman who was betrayed by Delilah and blinded by the Philistines?"

Speedy whooped. "Ease.Easy.Herc.Hercules."

"Samson is correct. Play or pass?"

"Fuck.Fuckin'ell.Get.Get'em'all,usuallyboy."

"They obviously haven't had your subject yet," Jones commented sarcastically.

"Load.Loads,boy.Hiss.History.That'smine."

"Next one to you Regina. What year was The Battle of Hastings?"

"Ease.Easy.Eight.Eighteen,something,seven."

"1066 it was. Play or pass?"

"Fuck.Fuckin'ell.Close.Close,though,boy."

"Oh yeah. Very close."

There was a faint jingling of keys at the front door. Speedy stiffened, glancing at Jones, who didn't seem to have heard it.

"Who.Who's,that,boy?"

"Huh?"

Speedy heard the front open, and shifted uneasily in his seat.

"Some.Someone,coming,boy."

Jones heard it now, and they both looked at the door.

Rosie, Jones short, plump sister, suddenly stepped into the room.

She looked at the scene before her, perplexed; at Speedy, at the television, at Jones, and back at Speedy.

"What the hell is *he* doing here?" she asked.

Speedy sat forward, gawping at Rosie pop eyed, swivelling his gaze between her and Jones.

Jones noticed the look on their faces, and laughed.

"Shall I make the introductions?" he drawled, smirking.

"Found yourself a new friend?" she asked sarcastically.

"I.I,bet,better,be,goin'boy," Speedy blurted, jumping to

his feet.

"Oh, don't leave on my account," Rosie responded caustically, folding her arms and watching him.

"See.See,ya,boy," Speedy mumbled, dropping his head, avoiding Rosie's eye as he darted past her.

Rosie stepped back a pace as he hurried past, looking at him like he was an apparition.

"Wadda you want?" Jones asked her coldly.

Rosie peeked around the door and watched Speedy disappear out of the front door.

"What the hell is he doing here?" she asked, looking back at her brother.

"Just visting."

"Since when?"

Grinning, he looked at an imaginary watch on his wrist. "Oh, he's been here about an hour."

Rosie blinked and shook her head. "Fine," she said irritably, "I don't have time for it today John."

"What?"

"Have you seen Timmy?"

"Why's everyone asking about Tim?"

"What do you mean? Who's asking about him?"

"He just was."

Rosie looked perplexed. "Was he?"

"What about Tim?"

"He's missing."

"Huh?"

"He's missing."

"Of course he's not missing," Jones scoffed.

"He didn't come home last night."

Jones face dropped.

"Nobody's seen him since yesterday. I haven't had a wink of sleep. I came around last night."

"When?"

"You'd passed out. I couldn't revive you. Did you see him yesterday?"

"Huh? Wha? You came around last – Tim's missing?"

Jones stared at the floor, unable to focus; his head pounding even more now.

"John? Have you seen him? Will you answer me. He's missing. Do you understand? He's missing."

Jones didn't lift his head.

The pounding in his head grew worse.

"John?"

Jones clutched his head. He heard his sister's voice dimly behind the pounding.

"John?"

In the corner, behind Rosie, Jones glimpsed a movement.

He saw Tim, head and face bloody, eyes gaping black holes, crawling toward him across the floor.

Rosie's tone changed. "John?"

Jones mouth dropped open.

"TIM," he shouted, lifting his stick, pointing.

Rosie glanced behind her, saw nothing, and glanced back at Jones in bewilderment.

"John?"

Jones watched Tim crawling closer, reaching for him.

He gasped.

"I'M SORRY TIM. FORGIVE ME."

With a strangled yell, Jones toppled forward out of the chair, dropping his cane, and fell face down on the floor.

When Rosie hurried across to her brother's side and

crouched beside him, she found him dead; his eyes wide open, lips twisted back exposing his teeth; staring into the corner.

"John," she whispered, "oh dear God, John."

10. BACK IN THE WOODS.

That woman walking in unexpectedly like that had shaken Speedy, just as he was getting comfortable too. He circled the block, passing Jones' door twice, before darting away.

He found himself at the edge of the woods, loitering near the path leading up into the trees.

He kept glancing pensively at the ominous gap, pacing, conflicted, smoking, until finally, weary of his hesitation, he threw his spent rolly to the ground and charged into the chirping shadows.

Ferns brushed his legs as he made his way deeper into the interior.

Then he saw it.

He stopped dead in his tracks, peering around nervously.

It had moved.

He could see a trail of blood; it had crawled a little way and stopped, face down in the dirt.

He edged closer. The small body was twisted, its jaw buried in twigs, the hair crusted with black blood, buzzing with flies. He prodded it with his toe to make sure it was dead, and it was like concrete against his foot.

The worrying thought – what if someone found it- again sent his searching gaze into the trees.

No one ever came out here.

In a few months the fog would roll in off the sea, stripping the summer outfits off the trees, and all the stricken leaves would bury it.

Then he froze, hearing faint voices.

Cold fear pierced his heart. In a bound, he hurried to a wall of vines and peered through.

There were two small boys strolling along the trail toward him, swishing sticks, laughing and chatting.

He picked up a large rock, determined to guard his secret.

They moved nearer, almost on him now; they'd see that dead Thing for sure if they came any closer.

He lifted the rock…

A distant shout suddenly sounded out. The two boys stopped and turned around.

"There they are," one of the boys said.

The distant shout sounded out again. One of the boys shouted back.

"Come on," one said to the other, and the two of them turned and sprinted back down the trail the way they'd come, whooping playfully.

Speedy crouched for a long time after they'd disappeared, clutching the rock, peering through the vines. After his hand began to cramp up, and he was certain they'd really gone and weren't coming back, he dropped it and stood erect.

"Fuck.Fuckin'cunts."

He went over to the dead Thing.

His hand brushed his trouser pocket and he felt something tickle his hand. Glancing down, he noticed the panties he'd taken from Jones' house the day before sticking out of his pocket.

Fishing them out, he pressed them to his nose and took a gargantuan sniff. The faint smell of perfume aroused him.

He looked down at that Thing in the twigs, unzipped his fly, took out his penis, and began masturbating, panting feverishly, pressing the panties to his nose.

Quickly, with a yelp, he ejaculated, his semen splattering the Things back. He wiped himself with the panties, and then, hesitating a moment, pushed them back into his pocket.

Zipping up, he checked the surrounding trees nervously, in case someone was watching through the leaves.

liss.listenmuh.mum…

Then he noticed the Thing watching him, its eyes following him from the twigs, the mouth twisted in a grin, laughing at him…

"Fuck.Fuckin,cunt," Speedy cursed shrilly.

He dropped to his knees and jabbed his thumbs into the Things accusing eyes; it felt disgusting, the matted, bloody hair cracking under his fingers. Whimpering, he pushed into the soft holes, blinding it. With a shudder, he fell back. The eyes were just black holes now, and it looked worse, much, much worse.

Clambering to his feet, he checked the surrounding trees again, terrified of being seen with it; That Thing and its gaping black eyes.

Someone would find it.

Someone was sure to find it – an old man walking his dog, a family picking blackberries, and those fuckin' kids were certain to come back again…

He had to hide it.

Grabbing its ankles, he dragged it into thicker brush, it's tiny, stiff hands grabbing at leaves and dirt as it moved, flies buzzing and trailing after it. He dropped it, fell to his knees, and began scrabbling at the ground, trying to dig a hole. But the ground was too hard and he gave up.

"Fuck.Fuckin'ell."

Instead, he desperately pushed leaves, twigs, and branches on top of it. When the obscenity was completely covered, a mound of mouldy leaves and twigs, he stood up, checked the surrounding trees again, and looked back down at it. It still looked conspicuous, the agitated flies stubbornly buzzing over it.

He checked his filthy hands, backed away, then wheeled around, and bolted, his legs thrashing through the wavering fronds.

Emerging from the woods into the open, he went home as fast as his legs would carry him, and when he got inside his flat, didn't budge.

Not until the morning, two days later, when the police pounded on his door.

esme

Patricia Hadley was profoundly disappointed when she smelled it.

She certainly wasn't surprised when her mother, who was standing beside her, made the inevitable comment.

"Uhg, smells worse than the last place."

"Mother," she reproached her, even though there was nothing to reproach her for. It *did* smell worse than the last place.

It reeked of stale urine.

"Well," her mother said, as though it was obvious.

"Let's just give it a chance," Patricia urged in a hushed voice.

"Hark at you," her mother tutted, "it wouldn't be you living here, *would* it?"

"Let's just give it a chance," she urged again.

Her mother pulled a derisory face.

Patricia gave an embarrassed little smile to the woman standing beside them; the allocation manager of the home.

Patricia was tall and gangly; her dark, greying hair cropped short, and wore round glasses, faded jeans and plain tops.

She took after her father.

Her mother was short and stout, and liked pomp and dressing up. She was vain with her hair and had it styled and set once a week.

A style Patricia called 'big hair.'

'You and your big hair mother,' she'd comment.

'Better than your borstal boy hair,' her mother would retort.

Her mother was leaning over, clutching a Zimmer frame. Her mind was as sharp as a pin, but her body was failing her.

That was why they were looking around yet another nursing home, or retirement community placement, as someone in the previous establishment had insisted on calling it.

Her mother was fiercely independent. She didn't want to leave her home of the last fifty years, but it had become little more than an obstacle course for her now. Even the stair lift there had become difficult for her to use, let alone the stairs themselves, which had become impossible years before. She'd agreed to look over some of 'those beastly places,' as she called them, but it wasn't going well.

'I'm not living somewhere that smells like a public convenience in India," her mother had stated repeatedly.

'I don't expect you to mother," Patricia assured her.

But here was another one.

"Would you like to follow me?" Elizabeth said brightly to them both. That's how she'd introduced herself to them. I'm Elizabeth, all friendly and welcoming, when she greeted them in the lobby. I'm the allocations manager.

Patricia gave her another little smile.

Elizabeth walked ahead of them a little.

Patricia bent down quickly and said in a hushed voice, in her mother's ear, "it's not always the place mother; sometimes it's just some of the people here."

Her mother swivelled her head and glared at her

daughter. "What's the difference? It still smells, doesn't it? Good grief." She shook her head at her daughter talking nonsense again. "Would you like it?"

"Mother!"

"Well, would you?"

"Let's just give it a chance."

Her mother gave a loud humph.

Elizabeth had paused before two large swing doors, waiting for them, smiling.

"Come along mother," Patricia hissed.

An office was to their left, the door open. Inside sat a silver filing cabinet, and a desk with a ringing telephone on top of it. On their right, through glass panelled doors, was a large room full of tables and chairs; the dining room. Doors to some of the ground floor residents' rooms stretched out in front of them down a corridor. A staircase, complete with a stair lift, was a little further ahead.

"Why doesn't someone answer the phone?" her mother complained. "It's like Piccadilly Circus."

"Come along mother," Patricia urged.

"Yes, yes," her mother snapped irritably.

She began propelling herself forward on her frame, pushing it, catching up, and pushing it some more.

"It does get quite noisy down here sometimes," Elizabeth admitted, "but it's very quiet in the lounge. And the rooms themselves are very peaceful too."

Patricia glanced at her mother. She knew that look. Her mother wasn't having any of it. That look said it all.

"This is the hub of it all, down here, the reception area," Elizabeth added.

The walls were covered in light blue, patterned

wallpaper. Watercolours hung on them, tasteful country landscapes of trees, fields and meadows. Little mahogany tables were dotted around, bristling with potted plants. The thick carpet was also blue, but darker than the wallpaper.

The wheels of the frame sank into it.

"The paintings are by a local artist, Myrtle," Elizabeth informed them.

Patricia's mother glanced up, frowning on hearing the use of her Christian name.

"May I call you Myrtle?"

"You just did," she snapped.

"We try to be on a first name basis here. We like everyone to feel like family."

"Isn't that lovely?" Patricia put in a little too quickly.

"I've already got one family. That's more than enough to deal with, thank you."

Myrtle stopped, huffing and puffing. The carpet was making hard work for her frame.

"Come along mother."

Myrtle glared at her, before shuffling slowly forward again.

"A local artist," Patricia perused the paintings on the walls. "Aren't they lovely mother?"

Myrtle paused again, lifting her head to take in the landscapes. "They aren't to my taste. Is the local artist who painted them a child, by any chance?"

"Mother!"

"Aren't I allowed an opinion?"

"Art is so subjective, isn't it?" Patricia grinned at Elizabeth.

Elizabeth smiled diplomatically.

Myrtle crept up to Elizabeth. She gave her the once over. "Have you got any children?" she asked.

"Yes," Elizabeth answered, "two."

"Are you married?"

"Mother!"

"What? I'm only asking."

"Yes, I am," Elizabeth answered.

"And would you like to live here when your family no longer wants you?"

Patricia tutted loudly.

"I'm sure that isn't the case Myrtle. There are lots of factors involved in wanting to house an elderly relative in a safe and secure environment."

"I don't know why you don't just send me to prison, in that case."

"Oh mother, really."

"It's hardly a prison, Myrtle," Elizabeth smiled.

"What do you know about it?" Myrtle asked. "You go home every night, don't you?"

"I'd be delighted to live here full time if I could," Elizabeth smiled.

Myrtle gave a dismissive sniff. "You would say that, wouldn't you?"

"Only because it's true," Elizabeth countered brightly.

Myrtle gave a snort.

Elizabeth pushed open the swing doors, stepping inside. "This is the lounge; we have Bingo in here twice a week."

Patricia and her mother exchanged a look. Myrtle loathed Bingo.

They paused on the threshold, surveying the lounge. It was a huge, deep room. A television sat in one corner. (It was difficult to tell what was on from such a distance). A dozen or more padded lounge chairs, all different shapes and sizes, were placed around, some occupied, some not. The carpet was patterned and red. More of the bland watercolours hung on the pale walls.

"Isn't it lovely," Patricia cooed to her mother.

Myrtle gave her daughter a withering look.

"There's another, smaller lounge we call the coffee lounge. We have coffee mornings in there every Tuesday and Thursday. But this is the main lounge. Most people call it the big lounge. The big lounge and the coffee lounge."

"How original," grumbled Myrtle.

"Coffee mornings, mother."

Myrtle gave a loud humph.

"Lovely and spacious," Patricia remarked enthusiastically, scanning the lounge.

"Some residents also have televisions in their rooms. The coffee lounge is also equipped with a splendid music system for our music lovers. Do you like listening to music, Myrtle?"

"She does. She loves music, don't you mother?"

Myrtle gave a tut.

Elizabeth added, "Some residents congregate in the lounges, others prefer to spend more time in their rooms."

"I'm not surprised."

"Mother!"

It smelled even worse in the 'big lounge'. Some of the residents (Myrtle hated that word, residents), were staring at them curiously. Some had obviously sunk beyond a trace into the black hole of dementia; twisted up into shrunken, brittle, grey parodies of their former selves.

Elizabeth said, "Hopefully you'll get a chance to chat with some of the residents later. Get some feedback first hand."

Myrtle glanced around the 'big lounge' at some of the blanket draped residents. "Are they capable of speech?" she asked.

"Oh mother, really." Patricia turned to Elizabeth, shaking her head. "I do apologise. Mother is a little out of sorts today."

"I am *not* out of sorts today," Myrtle countered. "And do not apologise on my behalf Patricia. I am not a child."

"Well sometimes you act like one mother. You can at least be civil."

"Shall we go and see the arts and crafts room?" Elizabeth interjected cordially.

"Shall we do that mother; shall we go and see the arts and crafts room?" Patricia barked, folding her arms, a sure sign she was working up a temper.

Myrtle answered, "I can't wait."

"Mother would be delighted to see the arts and crafts room, wouldn't you mother?"

"If it'll keep you happy – delighted."

Patricia let out a long, frustrated sigh.

"This way."

Elizabeth led them across the 'big lounge' toward another door.

"We have various activities in the arts and crafts room. It varies from day to day." Elizabeth struggled a little to recall the schedule. "Monday morning, let's see, we have painting; Tuesday afternoon, embroidery; Wednesday, model making…

"Which day is bomb making?" Myrtle asked.

"Mother!"

"That's alright," Elizabeth smiled, "a sense of humour is a good thing. I'm sure you'd get on very well with some of the residents, Myrtle. Some of them have got quite a way about them.

"Oh, I'm sure."

They exited the 'big lounge' and went down a hushed corridor.

"Here we are. It's ceramics today."

She opened a door and revealed a smallish room that smelled of paint. There were crude drawings pinned onto the walls, easels stacked in a corner, and a long, narrow, paint stained table taking up most of the space inside. Two shrunken men dressed in old, threadbare cardigans, and a very ancient woman wearing an apron, were dabbing at pottery with tiny brushes.

It reminded Myrtle of school. Of a time she had absolutely no wish to rekindle.

Elizabeth nodded to the artists at work.

"Albert, Ernest, Lavinia."

They looked up, smiling and nodding.

"How's it going in here?" Elizabeth asked.

A young woman appeared suddenly from behind the door, wearing a long, stained white smock, her long black hair tied back into a bun.

"We're just putting the finishing touches to our jugs. Hello there," she greeted Patricia and Myrtle.

"This is Megan," Elizabeth introduced them, "she runs things in here."

Patricia, grinning, peered around the door. "It's all go

isn't it."

"This is Myrtle," Elizabeth gestured.

"Hello Myrtle. Would you like to come in?"

"No thank you," she answered huffily.

"Why don't you go in and have a look mother?"

"I can see perfectly well from here, thank you."

"We won't bite, I promise," Megan joked,

Myrtle stood clasping the handles of her Zimmer frame, bored. Who did they think she was? An inmate in borstal? Arts and crafts indeed. Good Lord!

"We try to give residents a range of activity choices," Elizabeth informed them, "we try to keep residents stimulated."

Megan turned away, focused back on her charges, checking on their jugs.

"Isn't that wonderful, mother."

"If you think it's so wonderful, why don't you come and live here."

"It's just something that's available to residents if they feel like it," Elizabeth informed them, "it's entirely voluntary. For some people, it's more the social aspect of it that stimulates them. Just the chat and company they want. Some residents prefer to stay in their rooms and read. It's just an option."

"At least you'd have the choice mother."

"In all these years," Myrtle glared at her daughter, "when have you ever known me to be interested in ceramics? For goodness sake."

"It's not just ceramics – its different activities every day."

Myrtle pulled a face. "Model making?"

"It's just an option," Elizabeth put in, "it's not everyone's cup of tea."

Myrtle began backing up, dragging at the Zimmer

frame. Patricia and Elizabeth exchanged a look, Patricia raising her eyebrows.

"Shall we take a look at the residents' rooms?" Elizabeth suggested.

"Shall we mother? Shall we take a look at the residents rooms, since we've gone to all the trouble of coming here today? Since I went to the trouble of taking a day off work today mother?"

"I can't wait," Myrtle answered.

"Just follow me, please," Elizabeth suggested, stepping past Myrtle and leading the way.

Patricia bent down and whispered in her mother's ear, "You just aren't willing to even give it a chance, are you?"

Her mother glanced up, "What?"

"You just aren't willing to even try," Patricia said, disgusted.

"I just don't see the point in paying hundred pounds a week to come and live here to be miserable and bored, when I can be miserable and bored in your house for nothing."

"Yes, I see mother. Quite." Patricia folded her arms testily.

Here it was again.

Patricia knew her mother wanted to come and live at her home.

"I see mother. You agreed to consider it."

"I am considering it. I'm here, aren't I?"

It was Patricia's turn to give a loud humph.

Patricia's only child, Harriet, had just started her first year of university. There was an empty bedroom. The problem was that her mother couldn't use the stairs. This meant one of the rooms downstairs would have to be turned into her mothers' bedroom. It was possible, but not desirable.

Patricia's husband, Len, was easy going enough and would put up with it. He'd said, he'd go along with whatever she wanted. He got on better with Myrtle than she did. And there was already a downstairs loo. They'd have to hire a part time carer, someone to come and help her mother dress in the morning, that kind of thing. Her mother could pay for that. But it was the fact that her mother would be there, be there all the time; living there.

The thought was too much for Patricia.

Elizabeth was in the lift. She was pressing the 'door open' button, waiting for them. Myrtle felt the drag ease on the wheels of her frame as she left the corridor carpet and eased herself onto the hard floor of the elevator.

"This is the elevator," Elizabeth told them as the doors slid closed and sealed them into a hush. There was a slight jerk as the lift started up. "There's also a stair lift on the staircase."

"Isn't that wonderful mother. I don't have an elevator in mine."

Her mother gave her a look.

The lift was mirrored on its upper half. The three of them watched themselves as it ascended, humming, the cables rattling somewhere above them.

"Some people don't like elevators," Elizabeth said, "some people prefer to use the stair lift. Of course, you may end up with a room on the ground floor. At the moment, the only vacant rooms are on the first floor. That could change, of course."

"You mean when someone dies?" Myrtle asked.

"Mother?"

"What? I'm only asking."

Elizabeth cleared her throat, but left the question unanswered.

The lift stopped, shuddering a moment, before the doors slowly slid open with a hiss.

"This lift is safe, isn't it?" Myrtle asked.

"Perfectly safe. This is the first floor," Elizabeth informed them, stepping out of the box. She held the door as Myrtle slowly emerged into the corridor, craning her neck, glancing up and down, followed by a scowling Patricia. The corridor had a wooden handrail stretching along both sides of the wall.

"Let me show you the double first," Elizabeth said, unhooking keys off her belt.

"Double?" Myrtle snorted.

Elizabeth walked to one of the doors and slid a key into the lock. She opened it and led them inside.

The medium sized room contained two neatly made single beds, two small dressers, and a large brown wardrobe. A small portable television sat on a small table at the foot of one of the beds.

"This is a double," Elizabeth informed them.

"Isn't it lovely," Patricia commented.

"Good Lord. I've no intention of sharing," Myrtle exclaimed, horrified. "At my age." She blinked at the décor. "I couldn't live in here. Look at that wallpaper. And that tatty carpet. Good Lord!"

Myrtle began backing away, shaking her head.

Patricia folded her arms, colour rising in her face. "Well, I think it's a lovely room," she snapped.

"Some people prefer their own company," Elizabeth acknowledged.

Elizabeth locked the room and went to another door

opposite. "There'll be someone coming in every morning to help you dress, and someone every evening to help you prepare for bed."

"*If* I decide to move here," Myrtle snapped.

"Of course. If you decide to join us. All you have to do is pull the cord on the wall, and someone will be with you in a jiffy. Twenty four hours a day, in case you have any problems."

"Isn't that handy mother?" Patricia cooed, "twenty-four hours a day."

"This is a single, probably more your cup of tea," Elizabeth unlocked the door and stepped aside.

Myrtle peered inside. It contained a single bed, a chest of drawers, and a small wardrobe.

"Very neat, isn't it," Patricia commented, gawping over her mothers' head.

"What was it before, the broom closet?"

"Don't exaggerate mother. It's a perfectly nice room."

"You couldn't swing a cat in there."

"You don't have a cat mother."

"Good Lord."

"You'll have noticed my mother is very picky when she wants to be," Patricia said to Elizabeth.

"We all have our ways," Elizabeth answered diplomatically.

"Indeed we do," Patricia answered curtly.

"It's not the Ritz, is it?"

"Well, why don't you go and live at the Ritz then mother?"

"You've plenty of space in your house Patricia. That's all I'm saying. Perhaps it would be better for you if I just went to that clinic in Switzerland and had an injection. Perhaps that would be less bother for you all."

Patricia's mouth dropped. "Mother. Oh really."

Elizabeth stood with her hands clasped in front of her, listening, her big bunch of keys dangling from her fingers. She knew better than to get involved. She had another viewing after lunch, and felt it would probably be a better prospect than this one.

"Elizabeth has taken the time and trouble of showing us around. You could at least act cordially."

"She's only doing her job."

With a tut, Patricia said, "I do apologise Elizabeth."

Elizabeth shook her head, shrugging it off.

"Do not apologize for me Patricia, I've told you before."

"You really are too much sometimes, mother."

"Shall we take a look at the dining room," Elizabeth interjected. "You are booked in for lunch, aren't you?"

"Are we mother? Is there any point? Do you want to stay for lunch? Or would you rather go to the Ritz?"

"Well, now that you mention it, the Ritz."

Patricia shook her head.

Elizabeth locked up the room.

"What do your family call you?" Myrtle asked Elizabeth's back. "Liz, or Lizzie?"

Elizabeth stood straight, hooking her clinking keys to her belt. "No. Elizabeth."

Myrtle blinked at her. "All the time? Bit of a mouthful, isn't it. Elizabeth?"

"Oh, they manage."

"My sister was called Elizabeth. We called her Liz. Can't imagine us all going through life calling her Elizabeth the whole time."

"I've always preferred it," Elizabeth answered.

"Sounds peculiar, if you ask me."

"She wasn't asking you though mother, was she? Besides, you always call me Patricia. Everyone else calls me Pat, except you."

"What's that got to do with anything? We're not talking about you, are we? Not every conversation is about you, you know, Patricia."

"I'm just saying."

"I don't like Pat. It sounds crude. It was your father insisted on calling you Patricia. I've never liked that name. But your father had to have his way. Just to please some aunt on his side of the family. I wanted to call you Esme."

"Esme?"

"I've always liked Esme."

Patricia rolled her eyes, incredulous.

"I don't know what your father would make of all this business," she added, "not much, I'd wager. He'd be appalled."

"Shall we make our way to the dining room" Elizabeth murmured. "They'll be serving in a little while."

"Yes, *Elizabeth,* why don't we make our way to the dining room. I'm sure my mother would love to make her way to the dining room."

"You'll have to excuse my daughter," Myrtle told Elizabeth, "she's going through the change."

"Mother, how dare you. Really!"

"What? I'm sure Elizabeth has been through the change herself. Have you? How old are you Elizabeth?"

"Ignore her," Patricia snapped, "just ignore her."

"How old are you?"

"Just ignore her Elizabeth."

"I'd say, looking at that outfit," Myrtle glanced up and

down Elizabeth's light blue skirt and jacket combo, "you must be about sixty two."

"Mother!"

"I'm fifty four."

"Fifty four? You look older."

"Mother!"

"Has anyone ever told you Patricia, that you're like a parrot?"

"Sometimes I wish I was a parrot."

"Why on earth would you want to be a parrot? What a ludicrous thing to say. Especially as I'm the one being put in a cage."

"Shall we go and have some lunch mother," Patricia snapped irritably.

"If we must. What is it?"

Elizabeth slowly walked toward the lift, silently encouraging them to follow. She glanced at her watch. Time was pressing. "I think its Shepherds Pie today," she said to them over her shoulder. "All our food is prepared fresh, here on the premises. We have a wonderful chef. She's Polish. Many places have all their food shipped in by outside caterers. Everything here is made on site."

"Mother loves Shepherds Pie."

Elizabeth pressed the button. "I think it's the best Shepherds Pie I've ever tasted. Even better than my grandmothers; and I never thought I'd hear myself say that."

"Does she live here?" Myrtle asked.

"Uh, no. She's passed on."

They descended in the lift and emerged back on the ground floor. The phone was still ringing in the office.

"Why doesn't someone answer that phone?" Myrtle complained.

The dining room doors were wide open now. Some of the seats were already occupied. There was clinking and clattering coming from inside. People were shuffling in, some of them clinging onto the elbow of a carer, some being pushed in wheelchairs.

"Come on mother, let's get a seat," Patricia said, touching her mother's elbow.

"Would you please take your hand off my elbow, Patricia," Myrtle snapped.

"Heavens sake mother, I'm only trying to help."

"Make yourselves at home," Elizabeth told them. "I'll see you after lunch. It's all hands on deck during serving."

She gave a little wave and disappeared into the office. The phone stopped ringing a second later.

Myrtle pushed her frame, stopped, pushed, stopped, and slowly made her way over the threshold.

There were four long tables laden with knives, forks, napkins, and condiments. At the back was the kitchen area. Steam issued from a serving hatch. The air was pungent with the aroma of cooked food.

The smell reminded Myrtle of school dinners. Why did it all remind her so of school?

"How about there mother?" Patricia pointed at a chair.

"Not at the back. Let's sit near the door, please Patricia."

"How about here then?"

"Very well," Myrtle sighed.

Myrtle suddenly noticed a pair of scuffed brown brogues under her nose. She glanced up and saw a short, stout man, with one of the biggest bellies she had ever seen.

It looked like he'd put a beach ball under his pullover. He was about fifty; too young to be in an old peoples home. He was grinning at her, his yellow teeth oddly crooked. He had a pudding bowl haircut. Patricia pulled a chair free of the table before noticing him too.

"Hello there," she smiled.

He just kept grinning at them silently, blocking Myrtle access to a seat. He began making a gargling sound, rocking back and for on his brogues. Myrtle and Patricia glanced at each other with question marks in their eyes.

"Excuse me, young man," Myrtle said.

Drool began to ooze down his chin.

"Come along, Ronnie," a helper in a blue pinny suddenly appeared, grinning at them, gripped his shoulders, and bustled him away. He let himself be led to a seat not far away and sat down, still grinning at them.

Myrtle gave Patricia a sour look.

Patricia helped her mother sit, and sat beside her.

"Oh look, tomato soup," Patricia exclaimed.

Myrtle glanced up at the little blackboard above the serving hatch. Written in coloured chalk, the menu said:

Tomato soup; Shepherds Pie and Vegetables; Apple Pie and Custard.

Elizabeth appeared in an apron, carrying two bowls of soup, and put them on the table in front of two residents, before disappearing back into the kitchen.

A small, bent woman, with thinning hair died light blue that didn't hide the bald patches; her face heavily rouged; her lips glistening with bright, red lipstick, entered the dining room. She shakily moved with the aid of a walking stick. She came hobbling over to Myrtle and Patricia, glaring at them.

"What on earth do you think you're doing?" she asked them angrily.

"I beg your pardon?" Myrtle responded.

"This is my seat."

"Your seat?"

"I always sit there."

"No one said."

"I'm saying."

"I'm not moving now," Myrtle told her with finality.

"Are you new?" the angry little woman asked.

"We're guests," Patricia informed her.

She was appalled. "Guests?"

"Yes."

"Well, you shouldn't be sitting there. You'll have to move."

"My mother isn't moving anywhere," Patricia told her, "she just sat down."

"But this is my seat."

"We were told we could sit anywhere."

"Who told you that?"

"Elizabeth."

Even more appalled. "Elizabeth?"

"Yes."

"Well, she had no right. No right at all. This is my seat. I always sit here." She craned her neck, searching. Her voice became a high pitched shriek. "ELIZABETH? ELIZABETH?"

"Goodness me," Myrtle shook her head in dismay.

"ELIZABETH! ELIZABETH!"

"There's a seat over there," Patricia pointed at a vacant chair.

"That. IS. Not. My seat," she replied haughtily. "*You*

should go and sit there. *ELIZABETH. ELIZABETH."*

"Just ignore her mother."

"I intend to."

"ELIZABETH. ELIZABETH."

Elizabeth's head popped out of the kitchen, frowning, searching.

"ELIZABETH. ELIZABETH."

Elizabeth came hurrying over.

"What on earth are you shouting about Mary?"

"Ah, there you are. These people are sitting in my seat. Could you tell them to move."

"It isn't *your* seat, Mary. How many times do we have to go through this? There is no reserved seating in the dining room."

"But I always sit there. You know that. Why did you tell them they could sit there?"

"There is no reserved seating in the dining room."

"But it's my place."

"We've been through this Mary. There is no reserved seating in the dining room. It causes too many problems."

"But they aren't even residents," Mary complained.

"They're guests Mary. Please behave yourself."

Patricia could feel her mothers' eyes drilling into her.

"Well, I think it's terribly wrong. Not even residents and sitting in someone's seat. It shouldn't be allowed."

Patricia glanced at her mother. Her mother's expression was one of vexed amusement.

"Here, Mary. Let me help you to a seat." Elizabeth cupped Mary's elbow and began steering her toward a vacant chair.

"But that isn't even my table," Mary complained in

indignation, glancing back at Myrtle. "*That's* my table."

"Just sit down Mary, please. I've got to help serve lunch. I'm very busy."

"I think they should be thrown out," Mary sniped.

Another staff member came over and fussed over Mary as well. They coaxed her to sit, and finally, she shakily did, still demanding the intruders be ejected.

Elizabeth came across to Patricia and Myrtle. "I'm sorry about that. Mary's one of our more combative residents. Everything alright now?"

Myrtle answered, "Oh yes, fine."

"Fine," Patricia echoed, smiling.

"I'll bring you some soup," Elizabeth said, a strand of her immaculate white hair hanging loose over her glistening forehead.

"Thank you," Patricia nodded.

Elizabeth darted back into the kitchen.

Patricia could sense her mothers' eyes on her.

"Perhaps I could share a room with Mary?" Myrtle suggested. "Or Ronnie? Wouldn't that be nice?"

"Yes, alright mother. Point taken. I'll talk with Len tonight. Okay? Are you satisfied?"

Myrtle glanced across the table.

Ronnie, with his bowl haircut and beach ball belly, was staring at her, grinning. He poked his index finger up into his left nostril and twisted it around. Behind him, sat at the wrong table, Mary was still glaring at her in fury, complaining to another resident, pointing at her.

"...and she's not even a resident. She should be thrown out."

"Just one thing mother," Patricia said suddenly.

Myrtle glanced at her. "What?"

"If you do move in with me and Len, just don't call me Esme."

THE CONFESSION OF PAULIE PEANUTS

Father Vito Rozzi, a small, stooped figure in rustling black, checked his watch as he hurried across the cracked stone floor toward the confessional.

He was late.

One glance around his cherished, drafty parish of over twenty five years told him that, thankfully, nobody was waiting in the gloomy pews, not even Mrs Hernandez.

Mrs Hernandez was usually the first, and often the only, parishioner waiting.

Thinking it empty, he was surprised to hear a phlegmy cough from behind the closed grill as he stepped into the musty confessional.

It didn't sound like Mrs Hernandez.

He settled with a creak onto the seat, kneading his throbbing lower back, mentally preparing for the sins he was about to absolve.

Then he opened the grill.

The familiar face revealed in the lattice partition broke into a cheeky grin.

"Hey Choirboy, wudduhhear, wudduhzay?"

Choirboy…

A pounding chasm opened up underneath Father Vito Rozzi's feet.

*…Choirboy
choir-boy…*

He tumbled helplessly into dormant memory, into the corridors of Andrew J. McCorkle Junior High School, his twelve year old self in the school lavatory…

…his head being pushed into a stained toilet bowl, fingernails digging into his neck, shoved down and held while Paulie, laughing, pulls the chain, flushing the toilet, choking Vito as water goes up his nose…
'Yuh likedat choir boy?'…

Paulie's laugh, something like a staccato high pitched goose honking, echoed across the gulf of those nearly forty years.

Cold sweat broke out on Father Rozzi's forehead.

Stunned, he gaped at Paulie Gambini Jr.

"Heh, heh, heh."

…*that* laugh.

"Duntchuh recugnize yuh uld pal Paulie?"

Father Rozzi would recognise that face anywhere, *anywhere*, even after so many years.

…the toilet flushes again, Vito coughing and choking on the commode water…

Father Rozzi stared, speechless.

Paulie had inherited his father's dead eyes.

His hair was mostly grey now, thinner on top, combed

back neatly in the same style, imbedded with stiff, glossy comb marks.

He was heavier, his clean shaven, tanned face glistening like plastic; puffy black half moons under his eyes.

Deep crevices zig zagged from the corners of his eyes to his jaw line.

Half his left ear was missing, and there were white scars disfiguring his eyebrows, like some veteran pugilist.

His broken nose was broader.

He was wearing an expensive, dark purple suit, with a black shirt and a burgundy tie.

A diamond encrusted 'P' was displayed on a thin gold chain around his neck.

That sickening Smirk was intact.

How could his teeth possibly be that white, Father Rozzi wondered, *dentures?*

An overpowering, musky scent of cologne drifted through the partition.

That chuckle sounded again.

"Heh, heh. Yuh luklike yuh zeen uh ghozt Vito. Surry Vito, shud cull yuh Fadda now hah? Fadda Vito."

…'how'dyuh like dat choir boy?' Paulie taunts him. 'if Godz everywherz, hee muzbee dun dere too rite?'

'Wutz dat choir boy? Hay,' the twelve year old Paulie looks over his shoulder at his giggling, watching cronies to deliver the punch line, 'i dun dink hee likz' duh view.' Laughing, he shoves Vito's face back into the stained bowl and pulls the chain again…

"Paulie," Father Rozzi muttered.

"Heh, heh. Duhwun un-donli. Duhwun un-donli. Howzit goin Vito? Sorri. Fadda. Howzit goin Fadda?"

Before he'd dragged the struggling Vito across the floor by the neck, and shoved his face down into the toilet,

>...Paulie had taken a long, theatrical piss into it...
>...'heh heh'...

>...the 'water' is yellow and warm aromatic as Vito's face plunges in...
>'...come ere choir boy...'
>...choir boy...

"Gudduhgit uzed tuh zayin' dat. Fadda. Hah? Fadda. Gud fur yuh Fadda. i knuw yud make it. Gudfur yuh Vito. Meen Fadda."

"Paulie," Father Rozzi mumbled.

"Heh, heh. Yeh. itzmee. Heh, heh. Zuprized huh? How lungitzbin? Howlungzitbin Vito? Uh, meen Fadda."

Father Rozzi slumped, peering at his old tormentor, a knot tightening in his gut, his back throbbing.

"Yuh luk juzda zame Vito, uh, Fadda. Uh liddle grey izall." Paulie pointed. "Heh, heh. An duh X- ray specz ah, heh heh."

Father Rozzi unconsciously lifted his hand and touched his glasses.

"Howlung yuh bin werin' dem?"

"Glasses?"

"Heh, heh."

"Oh, quite a few years now."

"Dey luk gudonyuh. Diztinwizhed. Heh, heh."

A copious gift bag appeared behind the lattice partition. The hand holding the bag was encrusted with rings, one a prominent 'P'.

'Satriales' was written on the bag.

"Ma tort mee nevuh come empti handed," Paulie grinned, "yuh 'membur Ma Vit – uh, Fadda. Yuh 'membur Ma. A Zaint, shee wuz, a rul zaint. Yuh knoze." He waved a hand in the air, "Wutam-i-tellin' yuhfur."

…Paulie's mother, a Saint?…
…that broken, sullen, bitter woman…
…who in later years took to drink…

"Tort mee nevuh tuh bee uh schnorrer."

…schnorrer…

Father Rozzi smiled on hearing the word.

Hadn't heard it in years – a Yiddish word from their Old mixed Italian/ Jewish Neighbourhood…

…schnorrer…hah…

"Brut gifz fur miy deer uld pal."

Smiling, Paulie lifted a bottle of red wine from the bag. There was a crimson bow tied around its neck. He held it aloft proudly.

"Uh buttle ov Nero D'Avola Sicilia. Datz wur yuh peeple wuz frum, rite, Sicily? Mee? i'm Nabolidan, heh heh. Zo, tazte ov duh Old Country fuh yuh. Hay, i'm nuh exput, but dey tell mee itz one duh bezz. Datz wut dey tell mee. i'm azzumin yuh drink Vi- uh, Fadda. Nevuh met uh prieze yet didn like uh tipple, heh, heh. Doo drinkduntchuh Vito?"

Without waiting for an answer, Paulie put the bottle down and pulled something else from the bag.

A flat, slim package wrapped in white, waxed paper, tied up neatly with a bow of blue ribbon.

Paulie's hand danced in front of his face, his thumb touching two fingers in that oh too familiar way.

…heychoir boy…

"*Gabagool*. Duh bezz ah. Frum Duh Old Country. Diz'll meld inyuh mowt Vit- ah, Fadda. Meld inyuh mowt.

Hope yuhdun lizzen tuh deze crankz nowudayz badmouthin' ow fud, tellin' mee *gabagool* iz ull fat an whutzit, uuuh, nitratz. Nitratz, hah."

That chuckle sounded out.

"Heh, heh. Nitratz miy azz. Heh heh. if it wuz gudnuff fuh ow granddadz, den itz gudnuff fuh uz too, datzda Paulie philozophy."

Father Rozzi just stared.

…hey choir boy…

"Tuff uld bullz, bak den. Didn doo dem any harm, hah Vito. Tuff az iron dem old bullz bak den. Didn hur dem cumplainin' bout'nitratz. Yuh dun care bout dem doo-yuh Vito. Nitratz un shit?"

Paulie looked down.

"Uh, Fadda, i meen. Fadda."

Putting the *gabagool* aside, Paulie pulled another package from the bag.

A large triangular wedge wrapped in light blue, anchor patterned paper.

"Nowdiz," the fingers danced again, "diz iz duh bezz *Parmiggiano*; matured tenn earz in Duh Old Country. Sum uld widuh drezzd in black zat 'er fat azz on diz fur ten yearz ovuh der. Heh heh. Juz kiddin Vito. Like cheeze duntcha? Hope-zo."

Looking down, he produced another similar package, and held it up.

"*Pecorino dolce.* Hah? Duh bezz. Nuthin butduh bezz fur miy uld pal. Dun eet it dallut wunce dough ah. An duntake nuh notiz deze doom mongerz zayin' cheeze iz ull fat an, clrola-stirol, wuddever duh fuc – uh – wuddever dat iz. Lizzen tuh deze crankz an uhllyuh evur eat iz birdzeed. Like doze vegetarianz. 'Madjun dat, Vito, juz eatin' birdzeed an nuh meat or cheeze. How craziz dat?"

...HEY CHOIR BOY, GETDOVER HERE...

"Heh, heh. Wutz duh point inlivin."

Paulie grinned cheekily.

"i wuz gunna say, i'd getduh cheeze and *gabagool* induh fridge zoonzyuh can Vito, but itz zo culd inhur i dun dink yuh need tuh. Heh, heh. Yuh wunnuh getduh Vatigun tuh putt some heatin in here. Juz kiddin Vito, heh, heh."

Paulie put the *pecorino* aside and looked down into the bag. He pulled out a huge salami.

He smirked behind the salami.

"Ah. Heh heh."

His head tipped, came up again, "heh, heh," holding up a

rustic looking, dark green bottle with a long, thin neck.

"Wut kindov Italian wud-dye bee widout givin' yuh sum olive oil? Heh heh. Home made frum Duh Old Country. Yuh cun zmell duh fut odor frum duh *paesans* bin tredin on-it. Givz it extra flavur. Heh heh. Juz kiddin Vi – Fadda."

His head tipped.

Abruptly, he sat up again, his finger wagging at Father Rozzi in reprimand, "Hay, nunadiz stuffz frum Italianissimo, hah. Ull frum Duh Boot."

His head dipped again.

Next thing, he was holding up a white shoe box, and taking off the lid.

Nesting inside, peeping out, wrapped in fine white paper, were a pair of shiny, brand new black shoes. Paulie pulled the paper proudly aside like he was showing off his newborn baby.

"Han made in Milano. Bezz shooz induh wuld. Nex time yuh go tuh duh priezt ball, yu'll have duh bezz shooze inna place. Hadda gizz yur zize dough Vi – Fadda. Figure uh ten. Iffa dey dun fit, lettmee no, i'll change dem over. Yuh wer uh ten?"

"Uh, Paulie?"

"Hah? Yuh uh ten dere Vito?"

…hey choir boy, get-doverhere…

"Yuh uh ten?"

Dazed, Father Rozzi almost reached out and shut the partition.

But he'd never breached etiquette that way.

He wouldn't start now.

Not just because of Paulie Gambini Jr.

Who was smiling, holding up the shoes, waiting.

"Yuh uh ten? Wun i shud change'dem?"

Father Rozzi, clutching his knees, dropped his head for a moment.

"This is a surprise," he muttered.

"Hah?"

Father Rozzi, looking up, locked his eyes onto Paulie's, and repeated, this time loudly, "this is a surprise."

"Heh, heh. i bet." Paulie lowered the shoes. "Howlungzitbin?"

Father Rozzi shook his head. "I'm not sure. A long time. A very long time."

"Toolung, ah?"

Father Rozzi struggled to remember when he'd last seen Paulie. Thirty years…?

"Toolung-ah. How'd wee-let zo much time goze bi? Duh two ov uz wuz grate palz bak den."

…great
…hey choir boy, getdoverhere…
pals…?

The toilet at his Junior High School flashed through Father Rozzi's mind again. It had been one of Paulie's favourite ambush spots.

Throughout his youth, Father Rozzi's head had spent considerable time as an unwilling guest of various toilet bowls.

"Heh, heh"

…heh heh heh, take uh drink choir boy, heh heh…

"Grate palz, duh two ov uz, yuhan-mee ah, bak den."

…The Old Neighbourhood…

He was talking about the old neighbourhood.

Paulie lifted the shoe box high again.

"Wut 'bout duh shooz? Dye gizz rite? Yuh-uh-ten?"

Father Rozzi cleared his throat loudly. "I'm not sure it's appropriate Paulie."

"Huh?"

"I'm not sure it's appropriate."

"Wut? Shooz? Hey, leaze i didn brin no fizh, uh, heh, heh."

"Gifts in the confessional. It isn't usual."

Paulie waved his hand dismissively.

"Ah few gifz fur miy uld pal. Daz-ull. Don worri, dey ain bribz, heh heh. Bi-daway, duh Mazerati's park juz outduh bak. i'll leeve duh keyz widyuh wen i leeve. Heh, heh. Juz kiddin. Duh shooz-doe. Yuh-uh-ten?"

"Uh, yes," Father Rozzi answered.

He wasn't.

But it didn't matter.

He'd never wear the shoes.

Or touch any of the food and drink.

Gifts from Paulie?

No. *Never…*

"i'll put-dem induh pewz," Paulie said, leaning down, straightening up again, "wen were thruw."

Father Rozzi inhaled, trying to centre himself.

Centre himself in the here and now.

…heychoirboy…

He took another deep, surreptitious breath.

…heychoirb-…

"How'd yuh endup owt hear Vito? Owtinduh ztickz? Wutz diz church culled gain, Saint Barny Rubble? Heh heh."

"Saint Barnabus."

"Hooze dat guy? Heh, heh. An wutz diz town culled gain?"

"Dipton."

"Howduh endup owt here? Tort yuh'd bee Pope bi now, out-der in Rome, ridin round indat Pope Mowbeel. Heh heh."

"I'm not really Pope material."

Paulie looked offended.

"Hoo sez? Donchuh put yuzelf down. Lemmee talk-too-um. Yuh'd getmiy vote Vito."

"Happy right here."

"Or leeze wun dem Bishopz. Tort yuh might bee one dem Bishopz bi now. Wan i cumplain tuh duh Vatigun?"

"Not Bishop material either; just a humble parish priest."

"No wut yuh-ah? A Zaint. Yuh uh Zaint Vito."

Father Rozzi smiled. Paulie was handing out Sainthood to everyone, even him.

…heychoirboy…

"Hardly."

"Yuh wuz ulwayz uh inzpiration tuh mee Vito. Ulwayz. We ull lukked-up tuh yuh. Ullof-uz in Duh Old Neighbourhood.

Dat guy, i uzed tuh tell everywun, dat guyz-gunner bee Pope wun'deze dazes."

"I must be a disappointment then."

Paulie's face dropped.

"No-wayz. Yuh kiddin. Yuh gut digniti Vito, datz wut countz. Digniti."

Father Rozzi tensed, the knot twisting tighter in his gut.

What a word for Paulie to use.

Dignity.

…hey choirboy, getdover'ere…don't make-me fuckin' chaze yuh now…

…dignity?…

"Do I?"

"Yeah. Impotunt in life tuh have digniti. Datz wut yuh-gut Vito, digniti. Zowut if yuh ain duh-Pope. Hoo cirze?"

"Dignity?"

All that was a long time ago, Father Rozzi told himself,

…a long,
long time ago…
…focus…

Focus.

His thoughts instead drifted to his late father.

Paulie almost seemed to read his mind.

"Heh, heh. 'Membur datdump wee grew up in Vito?"

"How could I forget?"

"Membur dem wulls?"

Father Rozzi did remember.

Walls black with dry rot, and cobwebbed with thick zig zagging cracks.

"Yuh no dey pull'd datdump down."

"I know."

"Gud riddance, hah Vito."

They'd lived on the same floor, Paulie's parents and Vito's.

The old building they'd shared was a labyrinth of cheap apartments in a poor, shabby neighbourhood of Newark.

Paulie was one of Father Rozzi's first memories outside of his family.

He'd always been there, as present as the numbers on the doors, the rusty fire escapes, or those black, cracked walls.

Vito could hardly set foot outside his family's cramped apartment without Paulie grabbing him by the scruff of the neck.

He'd pop up from nowhere, like a ghost stepping out of the wall.

…heh, heh, gut any mony choirboy…

"I hear it's a supermarket now," Father Rozzi said.

"Datz rite. Ull newnow. Dey pull'd dat uld craphole ull down. i wen un wutched."

"You did?"

"Zat-der induh car widduh beer. Wutched em pull it down. Hated dat plaze. Hated dat plaze widduh pazzion."

Father Rozzi was surprised that Paulie would go and watch them knock that old building down.

"Didn tuk lung eider. Un our. Place wuz fallin dun anywayz. Had wun uh dem wreckin ballz. Zmash'd it tur rubble."

The buildings twisting, liftless, dim corridors, endless doors, and even dimmer staircases connecting the floors, floated into Father Rozzi's mind.

...his family's door number – 6-C...

Paulie Sr yelling through the walls.
A lot.

...Paulie's door number – 6-D.

They'd been neighbours for years.
"Kep uh chunk fur uh suvenir."
"Really?"
"Shudduh kep uh chunk fur yuh, Vito."
"The olive oil and the shoes were more than sufficient," Father Rozzi answered.
He'd meant it as a joke, but it came out sounding wrong.
Paulie's face dropped.
He scowled at Father Rozzi, drilling into him with those dead eyes.

...hey choir boy...

A twinge of the old fear stirred as if awoken from a long slumber, in Father Rozzi's gut.

...get dover'ere...

Paulie smiled.
"Heh, heh, ulwayz wuz uh jokuh Vito."

...hey choirboy, gut anymony...

"Dun fuget dat cheeze, heh, heh."

Long time ago, Father Rozzi told himself, *that was all a long,*

...long time ago...

He quietly sucked in a calming breath, thinking about that old slum.

Remembering things he hadn't thought about in a long time.

...mice in the cupboards...
...rats in the basement...
...leaking pipes...
...screaming through the walls...
...Paulie sitting on the stoop, smirking...
...Paulie's run...
...the way he'd drop into a crouch, frozen for a moment, then bolt, his beefy arms pumping in little circles, dead eyes fixed hawk like on Vito as, grinning, he closed in,
how impossibly fast he always was...
...heh, heh, come ere choirboy...

And all those years later, that same Paulie, sitting in his car, drinking a beer, watching his stoop being demolished...

What had been going through his mind as he walked over, picked up a piece of that destroyed place, and put it in his pocket for a souvenir?

"What did you do with it?"

"Wid wha?"

"The chunk of rubble?"

"Oh, dat? Onnuh shelv in duh bedrum. Nex tuh uh snap of Ma and Pa. Dey didder bezz, Ma and Pa. Dey didder bezz. Wuddunt der fault dat plaze wuz uh shithole. Time wuz hard. Time wuz hard." Paulie waved his hand. "Wuttum-i-tellin yuh fur."

"Hm."

Paulie's father gambled or drank away most of their money, as Father Rozzi remembered things.

And beat his wife, Paulie's mother, Livia. They could hear her screams and cries through the wallpaper.

Paulie's father, Paulie Gambini Sr, had been a 'wiseguy'.

(Nobody in the neighbourhood ever, *ever*, used the word Mafia).

Mobbed up, was the preferred expression.

'*A cheap, dime store pimp*,' he'd once heard his father hiss to his mother about the elder Paulie.

Rumour had it that he was a '*made*' guy, which in that mob world made him something special; part of the elite.

Rumour also had it that he wasn't a '*made*' guy at all, but spread it around that he was.

Whether it was true or not, he acted the part, strutting around the neighbourhood like a Little Caesar.

Father Rozzi just couldn't look at Paulie without seeing his father, Paulie Sr, especially as, *Lord,* he looked more like his clone than his son.

'Howyadoin,' had been Paulie Sr's usual greeting. 'Howyadoin.'

'...howyadoin kid...'

Father Rozzi's own father, Corrado, had driven a truck for a living, collecting dirty linen and delivering clean linen to bars, restaurants, and diners.

'*The working man keeps the clock ticking,*' was one of his father's favourite sayings.

...keeps the clock ticking...

A proud, quiet man.

Father Rozzi had only known him cry once in his life, reduced to tears by Paulie Gambini Sr.

That word crashed into him again – *dignity*.

Anger twitched in Father Rozzi's belly.

...long time ago.

...all that was a long, long time ago...

Focus.

...what could Paulie possibly want with me... after thirty years... thirty long years...

"Times were hard," Father Rozzi repeated, knowing it wasn't quite that simple.

"Pa ulwayz pud meat onna table, ulwayz pade duh rent, no mattur wut."

"Hm."

...whispers had it that Paulie Sr never paid a dime in rent in all the years he lived in that apartment...
...who would dare evict him...
...not a dime...

"Pa ulwayz pade duh rent. Ulwayz."

One of the things they did have in common, Vito and Paulie, was that neither of them had any brothers or sisters.

All the other Italian families around them in the neighbourhood were large, bursting with children and babies.

While they were both only children.

Another forgotten, ugly whisper floated up from Father Rozzi's memory.

...that Livia Gambini had been heavily pregnant with Paulie's sibling when Paulie Sr had, in one of his drunken rages, beaten her so badly she'd miscarried...
...leaving her unable to conceive again...
...marooning Paulie as an only child...

Father Rozzi recalled something else.

...locals in the neighbourhood used to call the elder Paulie, 'Paulie Fingers' (not to his face, of course), because of his habit of taking items from local shops without paying for them. He'd just pick things up, wave, 'howyadoin pops,' and strut out.
...Vito had seen him do it countless times...
...'howyadoinkid'...

Who was going to complain when confronted by those dead eyes?

Paulie Gambini Sr had lived in a different world to his blue collar, tax paying neighbours.

There were countless rumours about Paulie Sr, about his *activities.*

...that he was a pimp, ran illegal gambling joints, hijacked trucks, even that he 'wacked' people...

Locals treated him with grudging respect.

Respect and fear.

...'howyadoin kid?'...

...blind drunk in the middle of a working day...
...staggering home dishevelled on Sunday mornings as his neighbours were filing into Mass at St. Elzear, the local church...
...selling stolen booze and cigarettes from the trunk of his battered old car...
...shouting profanity while strutting around in his vest...
...kicking dogs...

Father Rozzi remembered it all like it was yesterday.

"Pa ulwayz pud meat onnuh table. He wuz uh Zaint." Paulie waved his hand. "Wuddum-i-tellin yuh fur. Yur knuw Pa."

Father Rozzi frowned in bewilderment.

Did Paulie *really* think his father had been a Saint?

...that thug...

When *Saint Paulie* disappeared into jail from time to time, the entire neighbourhood would breathe a silent, collective sigh of relief.

...stop the sarcasm, Father Rozzi reprimanded himself.

...St Paulie of China...

...Paulie would tell people his father was on missionary work in China...
...fully aware that everyone knew where he really was...
...proud of it...
...he was proud of it, his father being in jail...
...proud of it...

"The good old days," Father Rozzi commented sarcastically.
"Yeah. Heh heh."
Fishing a little, Father Rozzi said, "Bit off the beaten track."
"Huh?"
"Bit off the beaten track for you, out here in Dipton."
Paulie gave a dismissive wave of his hand. "Haf-an-our-onda highwaze. Nuthin too it."
"I'm honoured."
"Getouttuh 'ere. Duh honuz ull mine, ole frend."
"I'm trying to think when I last saw you, and I honestly can't remember," Father Rozzi admitted.
Paulie shook his head slowly.
"Life led uz dun diffrunt pathz ole frend. Yuh had yuh thin, i had mine." He shrugged. "Life? Wutahyuhgunna-doo?"

…different paths?…

Father Rozzi knew Paulie, just like his father, had been in and out of prison numerous times.

While Father Rozzi was studying in Seminary College, Paulie was doing time.

Different paths indeed.

…different worlds…

"Wutuhgunnadoo ah?"

…just behave like a priest…
…don't judge…
…(remember)I'm a priest…

"So when was your last confession?"
"Oh. Dat now?"
"Should I not ask?"
Paulie shrugged his purple shoulders.
"i'll holdup muh handz Vito, 'mit it rite offduh bat, i ain bin tuh Church fur yurz now. Ain cunfezzed uh nuttin."
"Oh?"
"Datz rite."
"Any reason for that?"
"Onacount uh Ma."
"Oh?"
"Member Ma Vito? She wuz uh Zaint."
"I remember your mother."
"Herd dat shee pazz'd?"

"I was sorry to hear about it."
Paulie suddenly glared, his eyes narrowing.
"Pose yuh wuz tuh bizzi tuh 'tend duh funeral?"

…why on earth would I attend your mother's funeral?…

"I didn't hear about it until after the funeral. Otherwise I would have."

With vague alarm, Father Rozzi realized he had just lied in his own confessional. He *had* heard about Livia Gambini's death.

…lied…
…in his own confessional…

Paulie's face softened.
"i no yuh wud, ul frend, i no yuh wud."
He waved a hand.
"Anywayz, Ma gut diz zenile dementurz."
"Sorry to hear that."
"Ain pretti, tell yuh dat Vito. Ain pretti. Tuh zee zum-one change like dat."
"It can be a shock."
"Tellin' mee. Ma didn evun no mee induh end. Didn evun know mee, her own sun. Bilieve dat?"
"It can be distressing."
"Ain pretti."
"Lucky she had you take care of her."
"Hey, i ain nuh bad sun. Datz uh dizguztin ting tuh bee. Bad sunz shud fuckin' die."
"Uh, – "

"Hadtuh pudder induh Green Grove. Herd bowrit?"

"Green Grove? An Old People's Home isn't it?"

Paulie tutted loudly, shaking agitated fingers and thumb in the air, before snapping irritably,

"Whyduh peeple dink dat? Itz nut uh uld peeplz home, itz uh retirument communiti. Green Grove Retirument Communiti. Nuttuh uld peoplz home. Duh bezz. Like duh Hilton fuh uld peeple. Coztz dough, ah," Paulie held up his forefinger and thumb and rubbed them together. "Ah, *Madonna*. Lotz uh dough. Nut dat i'm cumplainin. Diz iz Ma we're tukkin' bout."

"I've heard good things about it."

Paulie waved a hand. "Duh bezz. Duh bezz. Dey gut derown huzpital der an everitin."

"It's a challenge to see people change."

Paulie frowned. "Challunge?"

"It can sometimes test our faith."

"Huh. Tested mine, tellyuh dat."

"Did you seek guidance from your priest?"

Paulie plucked a comb from his breast pocket, ran it through his hair, and put it back again, patting his pocket, before answering, "Datz uh lung stori der. i did, but wut gud diddit doo."

"What's your priests' name?"

"Fadda Richie Aprile," Paulie answered, before dropping his chin and muttering something all but inaudible.

Father Rozzi just caught a, " – kin, -unt."

"I don't know him."

Paulie looked up. "An hee wuz Ma'z prieze, nut mine."

"He couldn't help?"

"Didn help nuttin wid Ma."

"Spiritually?"

"Widdher dementurz."

"But he isn't a doctor."

Paulie sneered.

"Huh. Stik up fur yuh own ah."

Father Rozzi frowned.

"What were you expecting him to do?"

"Help Ma."

Father Rozzi waited a moment to ask, "Do you believe in God Paulie?"

Paulie looked indignant.

"Wha??"

"Forgive me for asking. But it's a question sometimes I feel it's important to ask."

"Azkin' mee dat? Wadduh dink i-am, zum fuckin heathun? i wuz buptized yuh know. i wuz raized a gud cath'lic. Ma wuz rul strict bout dat."

"Do you still consider yourself a good catholic?"

Paulie gave a repentant shrug, his face dropping guiltily. "Zurry bout duh language, Vito."

He fiddled with a ring on his left hand. "Dizziz gettin' deep now. Unlezz datz uh trick queztion?"

"There's no trick questions in here."

"Well, puddit diz wayz Vito, I ain nuh Zaint."

Before Father Rozzi could stop himself, he snapped,

"Well, we both know that."

Paulie's head yanked back, his surprised eyes drilling into Father Rozzi's.

...one of Paulie's favourite pastimes (when he wasn't shoving

Vito's face into toilet bowls) had been punching Vito in the stomach...

...(remember) I'm a priest...
...remember...

He quickly added, "None of us are."

'...how'dya like dat choirboy...'
...Paulie clutches Vito's neck with one hand, dirty fingernails cutting into the back of his neck, while punching him with the other...
...again, again, and again,
slamming his big fist into Vito's belly, holding his bent, screaming body upright to stop him collapsing, 'heh, heh'...
...'heh, heh'...
...Vito dying...
...Paulie finally drops him...
...Vito collapses into a moaning, agonized heap...
...Paulie gloats over him, chuckling...
...heh, heh...
...'wherz Gud wenyuhneedim, hah, choirboy'...
...heh, heh...
...Vito curls around Paulie's feet like a wheezing, dying fish...
...Paulie's goons point, laugh...

...(remember) I'm a priest...
...a priest now...

Paulie's face twitched.
"Zuppoze nut Vito."

…except for your mother and father, of course…
…stop…
…stop the sarcasm…

"Did Father Aprile not offer you any spiritual comfort?"

"Wuzn' mee neezduh help."

"We all need a little help in that regard."

"He wuz Ma'z priezt, nut mine," Paulie mumbled sullenly.

Father Rozzi sensed rancour from Paulie toward Father Aprile, and decided to avoid the subject.

He shivered.

Paulie was right about it being cold in there.

"So how many years is it since you last confessed?"

Paulie shrugged. "Tuld yur. Nut since Ma. Earz go."

"You lost your faith?"

Paulie glanced down at the floor, scowling, fiddling with a ring on his left hand.

"Wutkinduh questionz dat?"

…hey choirboy, getdover'ere…

…Paulie perched on his stoop…
…Paulie's Stoop…
…'heh heh, dun forget it choir boy'…
…with his goons, watching, watching, perched there with his hunched, boulder like shoulders and thick, veiny arms like a giant, malevolent crab…
…always watching…
…clutching a bag of peanuts, ready to perform his trick, the trick that won him his name…

…Paulie Peanuts…

…dexterously flipping a peanut between his sausage fingers, across both hands, before crushing the shell in his right hand…

…'heh, heh,' and tossing the liberated nuts into his mouth…

…blowing the shell fragments into Vito's eyes, or dropping them into his hair…

…'hey choirboy, nuh wut dey cull deze in Eglund, Monkey Nuts, heh, heh. Monkey nuts. Bilieve dat'…

…(remember) I'm a priest…
…a priest…

"Ma turnd intuh veg'tuble. Wutkinduh Gud wee tukkin' bout here, letz dat happen?"

He glanced up, fixing those dolls eyes on Father Rozzi. "Tell mee Vito. Wutkinduh Gud we tukkin' bout here?"

…a priest…all that…
…all that…
…was years ago…

"These are questions human beings have been pondering since time began."

Paulie flinched in confusion. "Bout Ma?"

"About God, about life, about existence."

"Huh. Bud yur knowduh anzer, rite?"

"No. Only God really knows all the answers."

"Bud yur Gudz suldier dun here, ain yur?"

"Soldier? I would never describe myself as a soldier."

Paulie gave a dismissive wave of his hand. "Bud yur Gudz muthpeece dun here, ain yur?"

"Well – "

"Tuk fur him, rite?"

"I don't claim to have a direct line to the Lord. I don't claim to talk for Him. That would be blasphemous."

Paulie looked like he'd been slapped in the face.

"Huh."

"There's God and Good, and there's Satan and Evil, and in between are the likes of you and me, trying to make sense of it all."

"Huh. Da rite?"

"If you're asking me to explain what happened to your mother, where would I even begin?"

"Ma?"

"How can I explain it, let alone justify it?"

Paulie looked dazed. "Huh."

He shot Father Rozzi a suspicious look. "Yur ain lozz'd *yur* faith, haz yur Vito?"

Father Rozzi wondered if that's what it sounded like to Paulie; that he'd lost his faith? If that was the case, he wasn't setting a very good example.

"No. I haven't lost my faith." He made a lame joke of it. "Not yet anyway."

"Ull i azzed dat Aprile wuz tuh pud Ma outtuh her mizery. Daz ull. Shudda zeen her Vito." He dropped his shaking head, "bettuh tuh bee ded dandat."

"But how?"

Paulie lifted his head, snapping, "pray her ded."

…pray her dead…

"Datz wut priezt doo, ain it?"

Paulie held Father Rozzi's gaze.

Father Rozzi carefully considered his reply.

"Prayer can be very powerful, Paulie, but it's not voodoo."

"Hah?"

"A priest can't *pray* someone dead Paulie."

"Mubbee i shudduh tryed voodoo."

"I wouldn't recommend that either."

Hostile now, "Wut wud yuh recummend?"

"Faith."

"Faith? While Ma'z lyin' innur rown shit?"

"I know it's hard to understand."

Paulie's face fell into a contemptuous sneer.

"Shudduh nowd yud pazz duh buck Vito."

"What do you mean?"

Paulie didn't reply; just sat staring with that sneer frozen on his face. A brittle, hostile charge crept into the atmosphere.

"My own Mother died of cancer," Father Rozzi bluntly informed him.

Paulie's face dropped.

"Being a priest gives no immunity against suffering and death Paulie. Nobody is spared."

"Yur Ma dye-duh dat?"

"That wasn't pretty either."

After a long, uncomfortable silence, Paulie mumbled, "Surri bout dat Vito. i didn knoze."

...why would you...
...did you think to ask...

Father Rozzi couldn't help himself, "I thought I didn't see you at the funeral."

Paulie's left eye twitched, cords standing out in his cheeks as he clenched his jaw.

"Surri bout dat Vito," he apologised, but it sounded reluctant this time.

"Priests don't have a magic wand to wave around. Think I could pray my mother dead?"

"Surri Vito."

Father Rozzi tried pushing away images of his mother in the hospice, and failed; *oh Lord*, in those final, appalling days of her illness.

…pray her dead…

"Wish it was that easy." Father Rozzi heard anger creeping into his voice. "None of us are spared the realities of illness and death."

Paulie held up flat dinner plate hands, shifting back. "Poin takun Vito."

Father Rozzi took a breath, remembering how upset his mother would get when he returned home scuffed up and bruised from an encounter with Paulie.

"Poin takun. Nuh 'ffence."

…yuh gut dignity Vito…

Paulie dropped his gaze, fiddling with a ring on his finger.

"Yuh evur dink 'bout smuthrin yuh Ma widduh pilluh?"

Father Rozzi was taken aback. "Pardon?"

"Zeein' her like dat."

"Smother her with a pillow?"

"Dat ain nuh life."

"What are you saying?"

"Yuh evur dink bout dit? Derz wayz tuh dooit zo'z no-wun knowz."

"Paulie?"

"if i wuz indat state, i'd wunt zum-wun tuh smuther mee widda pilluh, tell yuh dat. Yuh nevuh tort bout it, wid yur Ma?"

"No. Did you?"

Paulie looked up, locking his eyes onto Father Rozzi's.

"Wutif i did?"

Father Rozzi said nothing.

Paulie was a murderer.

He knew that.

He'd heard the stories.

Paulie hadn't been convicted that last time, when there was all that publicity.

But everyone guessed he was guilty.

Considering the world he lived in, the people he consorted with…

…but his own mother?…

Paulie's dead eyes gripped Father Rozzi's.

…is it such a shock to imagine he could do it…

"Zum-wun dundat, atualli dun it, wut wud happun too um Vito?"

"It's a mortal sin."

Paulie frowned deeply, threw his hands up, looking away.

"Nut zayin' i dun it. i tort bout it dough. Dat wrung? Tuh dink bout dit? Wuntin' tuh pud zum-one outtuh der mizry?"

"It's not wrong to feel compassion for someone."
"Huh."
"So, we're just talking about *thinking* this, Paulie?"
Paulie shrugged, still not meeting Father Rozzi's eye. "Yeah. Juz dinkin bout it'zall. Zeein' Ma like dat."

…he just thought about, that's all, just thought about it…
…leave it alone…
…but I'm a priest…

Father Rozzi remembered the time he came home with a brand new shirt ripped almost off his back and a black eye; the starched blue shirt a birthday present…

…'VITO'…
…his mother, Isabella, wailed on seeing him…
…pouncing on his father as soon as he returned from work…
…'do something about it…
…look at this brand new shirt…
…Vito's eye…
…enough is enough'…

…'heh, heh, luk, duh choir boyz guttuh new shert, heh heh'…
…'hey choir boy, getdover'ere, heh, heh, letz luk ut dat shert'…
…at his mother's insistence, his father had gone and knocked on Paulie's door…
…knocked on Paulie's door…

Paulie dropped his head, pulling his comb out of his breast pocket and running it through his hair a few times before putting it back again.

Father Rozzi barely caught what he mumbled.

"...d duh biopsi."

"Pardon?"

Paulie looked up, "Hadduh biopsi."

"Oh. When?"

"Munday."

"Can I ask why?"

"Proztrate. Wuz havin problemz pizzin. Believe dat? Wutz it comin too, yuh cun evun take uh propur pizz nuh more."

"What was the prognosis?"

"Geddin dat tumorow."

...tomorrow...

A light bulb went off in Father Rozzi's mind.

...so, tomorrow...
...a biopsy result...
...I think I get it now...
...'Paulie only does acts of Paulie'...

"Doc zaze hee juz wuntz tuh bee shore, wid miy age un ull. Prubli nuttin."

"Are you worried?"

Paulie pulled a face and shrugged. He twiddled with the ring on his finger.

...his father knocks on Paulie's door...
...Vito stands next to him, his father's hand hooked protectively over his shoulder...
...Paulie Sr opens the door frowning, his hair an unkempt

mess, wearing rumpled red boxer shorts and a stained, torn white vest, scratching his backside, obviously roused from his bed…

"Yuh evur had wun o'dem proztrate exumz Vito?"
"No."
"Lucki yoo. Yur no dat Doc stuk hiz fingur up mi azz durinda exum. Bilieve dat? Hiz fingur? i don evun let sum-one wag der fingur inmiy face az uh rul."

Vito laughed.

Paulie's head jerked up, staring at Vito in surprise.

Vito killed the laugh with an embarrassed cough.

Paulie drilled those dead eyes into Vito, before his frown bloomed into a grin, those white teeth gleaming.

"Wud'nt wunt dat Docz job. Heh, heh, bilieve dat. A fingur up duh azz. Sum guyz owt der ud pay big buckz fur dat, heh, heh. imagine, doin dat all day lung, hah?"

"I suppose you get used to it."

Paulie looked appalled. "Hoo'd wunt too."

"It's good you can laugh about it at least."

Paulie shrugged. "Wudduhgunnuh doo? Hoo needz gettin uld?"

…'Wuh?' Paulie Sr grunts, blinks at Vito and his father standing there…

…Vito's father explains what's happened, holding the torn shirt up, points to Vito's black eye…

…an angry transformation comes over Paulie Sr's face…

…'Dis is why you woke me'…

…'Ya know it's futbull season right'…

Paulie's smiling face quickly fell back into a troubled frown.

"itz duh C wud wurryin' mee Vito."

"The C word?"

"Nut gunnuh zayit. Nut zayin dat wud. Bad luk wud."

"Did your doctor mention cancer?"

Paulie flinched.

"Pleeze, dun saze dat wud, Vito, huh."

"Sorry. Did your Doctor mention, uh, the, uh – it."

"Zaze itz probabli, uh, proztatitistis or zum'thin. Zaze itz probabli juz zwollen down der. Zaze der nuthin tuh worri bout."

"That's good then."

"if yuh stoopid 'nuff tuh bilieve dat. Wut elze hee gunna zay?"

...Paulie Sr, like his son after him, was a huge bear of a man, and towers over Vito's father...

...glares down at them both...

...'my busiest time, futbull season,'...

...Paulie Sr had gone to fat, his belly pushing out of the white vest like a beach ball...

...Vito's father ignores the comment, holds the shirt up, appealing for understanding, it's a birthday present, after all, the shirt, a birthday present...

...Paulie Sr's eyes grow wider and wider with consternation, then narrow to vicious slits, peering at Vito's father like a snake...

...those dead eyes had never looked more alive to Vito than at that moment, alive with hate and contempt...

...growing hot rage...

...Vito saw it coming but his father didn't...

"I'm sure he wouldn't lie to you."

"Huh. Everi-wun lize."

"Well, let's imagine the worst case scenario. Let's say the results come back tomorrow and you have it."

Paulie pulled back like he'd been slapped in the face, shocked. "Wha?"

"Just imagine."

"Dat i gutduh C wud?"

"Yes. Just imagine."

Paulie was mystified. "Hoo wunts tuh 'magine dat?"

"To prepare yourself."

Paulie stared at Father Rozzi like he was insane. Then a change came over his face.

"Ok," he agreed, "letz doo dat."

"What would you do if the results come back positive for, uh, – "

"Duh C- wud?"

"Yes."

"Datz wut i wuz gunna azz yoo."

"Me?"

"Wut yuh dink i shuld doo?"

"But why ask me?"

"Yur uh priezt ain yuh?"

"Well, I'd listen to my doctor's advice. Let him guide my choices. There are treatments."

"Nut azkin fur medicul avice. Can getdat frum duh Doc."

"What advice are you asking?"

"Priezt avice. Datz why i come on dun here tuh zee yuh. Hoo better tuh azz dan miy uld pal Vito."

"Okay. That's flattering, though any priest would advise you as well as myself, I'm sure."

Paulie waved a dismissive hand. "Huh. Like dat Richie Aprile? Guy wuz uh azzhole. Wearin' uh doggie collur ain proof 'gainz bein an azzhole. Nuh uffence Vito."

"You're right. Wearing a dog collar doesn't make us Saints."

"Huh. Tellin' me."

…that's right, remember,
I'm a priest…
…here's a sinner come looking for God…
…even if it is Paulie…
…(Paulie only does acts of Paulie)…

"Are you here to atone for your sins?"

"Wha?"

"Are you here for penance?"

"Penunce?"

"Yes."

"Wut iz dat anywayz, penunce?"

"Penance? Well, it can be voluntary self punishment to atone for a sin."

"Huh."

"A feeling of regret for one's wrongdoing."

"Huh."

"A sacrament in which repentant sinners are absolved on condition of confession of their sins to a priest."

"Huh."

"I sound like a dictionary."

Sounding none the wiser, Paulie asked, "Datz penunce?"

"Are you here to confess your sins?"

"Ull lovum?"

"That's up to you."

"How lung yuh gut, heh, heh."

…remember, I'm a priest…

…'wut ya bring dat kid fur, tuh hide behine'…

Paulie dropped his head, face hidden under those grey glossy comb marks, fiddling with his ring again.

"Treetmunt yuh juz sed?"

"Yes. There are treatments for can -, uh, if, uh – there are treatments."

Without looking up, Paulie mumbled, "Didyuh evur knoze Dominic Tedesco?"

"Dominic Tedesco? No. Was he from the old neighbourhood?"

"Nah. i dun dink yuh knuw Dom. Big Dom Tedesco. Frum North Caldwell. Two ov uz run uh whorehouze fur 'wile in A.C." Paulie paused, a flash of consternation on his face as he looked up. "Huh. Itz ok tuh tell yuh dizstuff, ain it?"

"I've heard a lot in this confessional over the years, believe me."

Paulie grinned. "i bet. Yuh gettuh hare itall, huh. No 'vryone'z secretz, heh heh."

Father Rozzi quickly chipped in, "But I'll never tell."

Paulie nodded, half smiling, half confused, not quite sure how to take the remark.

"Huh."

"Go on."

"Huh?"

"Atlantic City."

"Oh, yeah. Zo. Big Dom Tedesco. Mee an' him in A.C.

fur awile der. Big Dom. Huge diz guy, like a fuckin' tree. Mee, hadduh luk up tuh tuk tuh him. An' i ain no midjet. Anywayz, hee gutz it. Duh C wud. Hee gutz it. Big Dom."

Paulie shook his head gloomily.

"Tuk bout treetmuntz. Fuckin' keemo. Treetmuntz wurze dan duh dizeeze."

Paulie fell silent, thinking, and Father Rozzi didn't interrupt his recollections.

"Gut'dit bout five yearz 'go, duh C word, Big Dom der. Nevur zick uh day in hiz life 'for dat.

Father Rozzi heard such things all the time. Usually it wasn't true.

"Gud palz, Big Dom an mee. Bull, king ov duh rodeo fuckin bull hee wuz. Den hee getz it. Duh C wud. How come Gud make'z zumthin like dat? Huh? How come Gud creatz dat Vito?"

"Can? – "

Father Rozzi stopped himself from saying the forbidden word just in time.

Paulie waved his hand in the air. "i knoze wut yuh gunnuh sayz. Duh Devul, right. Ull duh bad stuff getz blamed onduh Devul."

"Well, it's – "

Paulie held his dinner plate hands up. "Hay, i ain blamin' yoo."

Then dropped his head, fiddling with his ring again.

"Anywayz, Dom Tedesco getz it. Duh C wud. Guzz intuh duh huzpitul. Haz dat keemo ting," he looked up, pointing accusingly, "onhiz Docz 'dvice, diz iz, mind, ah. Onhiz Docz 'dvice. Doctorz, ah? Wut kinduh purzun wuntz tuh spen der life touchin' strangerz ull day lung, datz wut i'd like tuh know?

'Magine dat?"

Before Father Rozzi could reply, he went on,

"Zo Dom haz duh keemo. Haz whutever 'iz Doc sayz tuh git." Paulie jabbed his big thumb into his chest. "i goze tuh zee 'im." He flinched back, eyes popping wide. "*Madonna.* Didn't evun knoze it wuz Dom. Didn recugnize him. Wulked in lukkin' fur diz fuckin tree, couldn zee 'im anywherze. An hee wuz right unduh my noze der, juz didn recugnize 'im. Fuckin' keemo srivelled 'im tuh nuthin." He dipped his head, taking out his comb, and ran it through his hair quickly, before putting it back in his breast pocket. "Lozz ull hiz hair too, ah. Buld az uh babiez azz. Keemo srivelled 'im tuh nuthin." He held his hands clawed around his cheeks. "Bud wid dat big face ah."

"Moonface?"

"Dat wut dey cull it?" Paulie shuddered. "Moonface? Huh. Know wut he lukked like? Lukked lik wun 'dem stale pretzelz uld man Jack uzed tuh zell on 'iz cart onnuh cunnur bak den. 'Member Vito? 'Member, bak in duh Old Neighbourhood? Uld man Jack. Jack Massarone?"

A figure popped into Father Rozzi's mind like a long forgotten photograph he'd pulled from a drawer.

…Old Man Jack Massarone…
…haven't thought of him in years…
…Old Jack Massarone…

"'Member dat uld cartduh iz, heh, heh?"

…a small, bent, brown man with a weather beaten, deeply etched face…
…a large Roman nose jutting out of a small, ancient head

always adorned with a tilted, black beret...

...always wore old black trousers held up with frayed pale string...

...that old cart of his, with a torn, ineffective, black umbrella fluttering over it...

...just a trolley, selling lemonade and snacks...

...the start of summer was always heralded by Old Tony parking that trolley on the corner and shouting his gobblygook greeting to the neighbourhood, 'anassdapidonaaaa', it sounded something like, 'anassdapidonaaaa'...

...no one ever knew what it meant...

...his home made lemonade was always fresh and zesty, kept chilled by a block of ice that would melt as the day went on, slivers of it plonked into glasses by his gnarled fingers adorned with red bumps...

...sometimes Old Jack would send one or two of the neighbourhood kids for the ice in exchange for free goodies off his stall...

...Father Rozzi had gone a couple of times himself...

...for free lemonade, not snacks...

...if Jack pushed any snacks onto him, he'd stuff them in his pocket and bin them later...

...they were always stale, rancid...

...Jack kept them exposed to the sun, and the flies, all day long...

...there'd be clusters of tiny white eggs on them...

...some people actually ate them without realizing...

...Old Jack spoke Italian most of the time, and when he spoke in his broken English, sounded like Chico Marx...

...'yooo-ah take-uh, ah, four your fard-ar, four your fard-ar'...

…Old Man Jack Massarone was the only person Paulie Sr always paid if he stopped by his stall…

…Old Jack's wriggling, twisted red bumpy fingers would tap Paulie's Sr's arm for the money, and stay there until the money was handed over…

…he was the only person in the neighbourhood Father Rozzi had seen clip 'his' Paulie across the ear…

…Paulie and some of his goons were hanging around Jack's trolley one afternoon clowning, until Jack's hand shot out, slapping Paulie across the back of the head hard enough to knock his head forward and bring all the boisterous clowning to dead silence…

…Paulie was already as big at that tender age as Old Jack and swung around glaring at his elderly assailant, stepping toward him threateningly, his jaw locked in fury…

…Old Jack didn't flinch, just grinned, 'tuf-fa guy hah?'…

…Paulie glared, murmured 'dun mezz widduh hair popz' and walked off, pulling his comb from his back pocket and running it through his hair as he motioned his goons to follow…

…'scumpari chiacchierone', Jack called after him, then holding his nose he called, 'chepuzzo' and finally, tapping his fingertips to his lips, 'pucchiacca'…

"'Membur Vito?"

"Old Man Jack? What a character."

"Yeah. Der'ull gun now. Ull dem Old Timerz frum duh Boot." Paulie waved his hand impatiently. "Anywayz, why we tukkin' 'bout Old Jack?"

He answered his own question. "Dun wunna dink bout Dom izall, lyin' der lukkin' like dat. Firz Ma, den Dom." He shook his head. "Nevuh wen bak tuh see Dom 'gain. Lukk lik uh fuckin mummy, Vito. Bilieve dat. One dem mummyz frum uh uld horror flick. Den, aftur ull dat treetmunt hee had, Dom, hee died uh. Zo itwuz ull fur nuttin."

"I'm sorry for your loss."

Paulie's lip curled. "Hee wuz bettur uff, bilieve mee, hah. Bin bettur uff havin' nunnuh dat keemo crap."

"But some people recover."

"Hah. Telldat tuh Dominic Tedesco."

"What was the alternative?"

Paulie shrugged. "Wut wud be?"

"What do you mean?"

"Dem treetmuntz uh deth zentince Vito. Yuh evur come 'cross Rocco Dimeo? Ulwayz uzed tuh wer diz grate jackit."

"Rocco Dimeo? No, no, I don't believe so."

"Uzed tuh box. Cudduh bin wunov duh bezz middlewaitz round iv he'd wunted tuh bee. Hoo wuntz tuh bee uh boxer, dough, huh? Marquiz ov Queenzbury rulz." He snorted in contempt. "Gimmee uh brake.

Ull dat trainin', ull doze zweaty, zmelly gymz? Tellin' yuh nut tuh fuc – uh, get laid. Wimen weaken legz, hah. Zo wut?" Paulie pointed an advisory finger at Father Rozzi. "Bee uh manuger, yuh wunt tuh git 'volved induh ring. Datz mi 'dvice. Fightinz uh mugz game. Shud zeezum deze punch drunk zombiez aftur uh life inda ring." He stopped, then added, "i hadduh pieze ov uh fightur wun time."

"Oh?"

"Diz guy," Paulie waved his hand with a snort, "wudn take uh dive wen he wuz tuld, uh."

"A dive?"

"Hey, itzall part tuh duh game Vito. Yuh take uh dive wen

yuh tuld indat game. Nut evun gunna tell yuh wut happn' tuh dat guy."

"Why not?"

"Ain impotunt. Lezz juz zay hee nevur box'd 'gain."

…I bet he didn't…

"You used to box, didn't you?"

Paulie held up a looped finger and thumb. "Little bit. Gave it up 'fore i lozzed my gud luks, eh, heh, heh. Mugz game, duh fightz. Why wuz i tulkin' bout dat anywayz?"

"Rocco Dimeo."

"Hah? Oh yeah. Rocco Dimeo. Dat grate jackit. Nah, yuh wuddn' knozed Rocco. Hee wuz'n frum duh Old Neighbourhood. Uzed tuh run numberz in Jerzey City. Gud pal mine fur yerz. Did uh stretch tugether in County. Rocco, hee gut it too, duh C-wud. Believe dat? Zame ding happn' tuh Rocco. Tunned intuh wunov Old Jackz pretzelz. Eaten 'way. Juz like Dom Tedesco. Aftur dat fuckin keemo. Tankz tuh dem docz an der 'dvice."

…'wut yuh hidin' behine dat kid fur?'…

"But what's the alternative?"

Paulie shrugged. "Datz why i come here tuh zee yuh fur."

"What do you mean?"

Paulie stared back at Father Vito, those dead eyes as close to fiery life as Father Rozzi had ever seen them. Cords pulsated on the clenched cheeks of his jaw.

…Vito could see it coming…

…'wut yuh hidin' behine dat kid fur'…
…but his father didn't…

Paulie suddenly opened his mouth, imitated a gun with his right hand, and put the tip of the 'gun' into his mouth, moving the thumb down to imitate the 'gun' firing.

Then he took the 'gun' out of his mouth.

"Game ovur," he snapped.

Father Rozzi let it sink in.

"Wudduh yuh dink uhdat?"

"I see."

"if i goze tuh duh Doc tumurow, an i gut it, duh C-wud, why shudn i, Vito, huh?"

"Tomorrow?"

"Nutdat, no. Bud wen duh time comz. Wen duh time comz."

"That's your intention?"

Paulie shrugged. "i ain bin 'fraid o'many thins Vito, in diz crazi wuld, but seein' Dom eatun 'way like dat, den Rocco Dimeo. And Ma. *Madonna*. Hoo wuntz dat?

Dom Tedesco wuz like uh fuckin' tree. Nex thin' he'z turn'd intuh wun uh Old Jackz pretzelz." Paulie dropped his face into his hands.

…strange, to see Paulie afraid…

"It's natural to be afraid," Father Rozzi told him, meaning to be comforting.

Paulie's head jerked up, indignant, glaring.

He'd taken it as an insult somehow, even after what he'd just said.

"Dat rite?" he snapped with hostility. "Yur 'fraid ov dyin' Vito?"

After a moment's hesitation, he answered, "Yes. Yes I am."

Paulie looked confused. "Bud yuruh priezt aintcha?"

"Doesn't mean I'm not afraid."

"Budchuh goin tuh hevun, aintcha?"

"I'd like to think so."

"Wut yuh 'fraid ov, den?"

"The unknown, I suppose."

"Unnown? Wuttuh bout duh Bible? Ull in der ain it?"

"I wonder?"

"Huh?"

"Priests fear death too; some of us anyway."

Paulie frowned.

"You think you'll go to heaven, Paulie?" Father Vito asked.

"Shure. Why nut?"

"Suicide is a mortal sin."

…alongside the other mortal sins you've undoubtedly committed…

Paulie eyes narrowed, lines cutting deeper into his face.

"Datz why i comz tuh zee yuh. Mubbee wee cancome tuh zum arangemunt."

"Arrangement?"

"Yuh bein' uh priezt un ull."

"I don't understand."

"iffuh i doo dat ding," Paulie held up the 'gun' again, "mubbee yuh can wutch miy bak widduh Big Guy upstairz."

"I don't quite know what you mean."

"Yuh cun make it ok."

"How?"

"Whyzit uh mortal sin, tuh doo dat, anywayz?"

"Life is sacred."

"Bud itz miy life, ain it?"

"It belongs to God."

"Hah. Dat rite? Zo, itz ok tuh getduh C –word, an spend munthz in aguny gettin' eetun 'way like Dom? Like Rocco Dimeo? How come dat ain uh mortul zin?"

"It isn't suicide."

"Bud yuh end up ded one wayz or duh-udder, dontcha? Wutz duh diference?"

"Suicide is the difference."

"Zo, itz ok fur mee tur die screamin' in aguny like Dom, butt nut tuh doo myzelf in?"

"Well ,basically, yes."

"Hah. Wut kinda Gud we tulkin' 'bout here?"

"Well – "

"Zo, Gud wud raddur zee mee dye uh slow, painful det dan uh quik, painlezz one?"

"I wouldn't put it quite like that."

"How wudd yuh pud-it?"

"There are drugs to ease your pain, aren't there."

"Zo, itz ok tuh bee uh junki. Gud wantz mee tuh bee uh junki now?"

"It's not about being a junkie. Drugs are just a tool to be used, a tool to ease your pain, aren't they?"

"Why pud up wid it attull. Wut fur? it ain like yuh gunna git beddar, izit."

"Though shalt not kill."

Paulie shook his head. "Datz crazi. Wut kinduh Gud wee tukkin' bout here?"

"Perhaps you should make a full confession. That might be a start, since you're here. Try and bring yourself closer to God."

Paulie looked stunned. "Full cunfession?"

"It might be a start."

"Stat uh wut?"

"Bringing you closer to God."

"Hah. Dat rite?"

"You need to vocalise."

"Wuttam i, Sinatra now?"

"Bare your soul to God."

"Full cunfession?" After a short pause, he added, half heartedly, "How lung yuh gut, heh, heh."

"What happened to your ear?

Paulie lifted his ring adorned hand and touched his half ear.

"Dat? Yuh wunnuh no bout dat?"

"Only if you feel comfortable talking about it."

"Hah."

"You didn't have it last time I saw you."

Paulie shrugged. "it wuz Culumbianz."

"Columbians?"

"An' deze two doosh bagz, Matthew Bevilaqua and Sean Gismonte. Laurel and fuckin Hardy doze two."

…no apologies for the profanity now…

"I don't know them."

With disdain, he answered, "Yuh wudn't no dem. Dey ain 'round nuh muh anywayz."

"Oh?"

"Dey pudmee ontuh diz Culumbian lundry in duh nayborhud."

"Columbian laundry?"

Father Rozzi pictured a Laundromat with aisles of washing machines and tumble driers spinning clothes.

But a *Columbian* laundry?

He had a feeling something else was being discussed.

"Are we talking about a *laundry* laundry?"

Paulie gave him a look.

"Tukkin' bout drug munny. Culumbian drug munny."

"Oh."

Paulie pointed an angry finger, "Dey had nuh biznezz bein der. People gut nuh rezpect deze dayz. Dey new whoze nayborhud dey wuz in. Hordin cash didn't belung tuh um. Nut indat nayborhud. Itz duh wild wezt outder deze dayz. Ain like bak in ow day Vito." Paulie held up his hand and began counting off one finger at a time, "Yuhgut Culumbianz, Cubanz, Ruzzianz, Albanianz, Koreanz," he threw his hand up in despair, "plenti uv utherz too, ull wuntin uh pieze uv wut wee gut."

Paulie looked hard at Father Rozzi.

"Guttur un'ztan', i'm uh zoldier Vito. i'm outder fightin' uh wur."

"A war?"

"Datz right." He touched his half ear. "Diz iz uh wur woond. Shud ov gut uh medul fur diz."

"War wound?"

"Datz rite. Dey ull wuntuh pieze ov uz. Comin' intuh ow patch, dinkin dey cun take over. Huh! Dink gain hah." After a slight pause, he continued with pride, "it wuz Italianz bilt diz cuntry. Wut wud diz cuntry be widdout Italianz, huh. Italian fud, an ar paintinz, an ar clothz, ar coffee, ar buildinz, an ar savvy, huh? Dey wuz eatin' garbage fur wee come over here. An yooze lot too, bringin reeligin tuh deze fuckin heathenz." He flipped a hand in the air. "Wutam-i-tellinyuhfur."

"Many cultures have helped shape America."

Paulie pulled a derisory face. "Wut? Duh niggerz an wetbackz? Wut dey dun fur diz cuntry?"

"I'd rather you didn't use such words in here Paulie," Father Rozzi snapped irritably.

Paulie froze, annoyed. A tension crept into the air.

"Heh, heh." Paulie smiled.

"Heh, heh." The tension popped like a soap bubble. "Fare nuff Vito. Yuh guttuh doo yuh jub. Ull i'm zayin' iz Italianz made diz cuntry. Yuh know i'm rite. Lukkat yuh Pa. Hud wukkin' men like yuh Pa bilt diz cuntry."

…the working man keeps the clock ticking…

"Men like yuh Pa, un mine, bilt diz cuntry. Yuh 'member miy Pa Vito. Hee wuz uh Zaint." He flipped a hand in the air. "Wutam-i-tellinyuhfur."

…Vito saw it coming…
…'wut yuh hidin' behine dat kid fur'…
…but his father didn't…

…a Saint?…

"You were telling me about your ear," Father Vito prompted him, trying his best to ignore the anger he felt flickering inside him.

"Huh? Oh yeah. Yuh wuntz tuh knoze bout dat." He touched his ear again. "Doze two doosh bagz, Matthew Bevilaqua an' Sean Gismonte. Dey wuz zuppozed tuh scout dout diz Culumbian lundry. Der job ah. Tuh scout duh place dout. itz cuz-uh clownz like deze two we're lozin' groun' outder." Paulie extended his index finger from a raised fist. "Wun personz zuppozed tuh bee indat lundry. Datz wut deze two clownz tul mee. Wun personz." He gave an exasperated shrug. "Zo, wee goze inder. *Madonna*. Der wuz uh fuckin' armi inder. i'm lucki diz-iz ull i lozzed. Doze two clownz were'n zo lucki. Dey gut der ticktz punched. Servz der fuckin rite. Uzed wun dem fur uh sheeld, hah."

"They were killed?"

Paulie spread his arms wide in celebration, smirking. "Yuh lukkin at duh laz man standin' frum dat day."

Father Vito said nothing, trying to picture the situation Paulie was describing. A superficial scene, like something from a Hollywood movie, popped into his mind. But he couldn't really imagine it at all.

Not really.

"Shot miy ear uff dough. Datz wut happen'd der. Wudduh dink-uh-dat?"

"How many men were killed?"

"Wuzzn juz men. Der wuz wimmin der to, ah. Doze spickz wuz havin' uh parti." He shrugged. "How menni? Hoo knoze? Didn stup tuh count. i found duh munny in duh end? No were? in-duh wushin' machine, heh, heh, zo it rully wuz uh lundry."

After a short pause, happy with himself, he asked, "Diz duhkinduh ding yuh wunt? Diz gunna gettme clozur tuh Gud?"

"Only if you show contrition. You must make an

effort to embrace the church. You're in a state of mortal sin. Sin is an offence against God. You're disobeying his commandments. You must feel contrition."

...is he carrying a gun right now...

Paulie frowned. "Yuh mean i'm suppozed tuh feel zurry bout it? Hey, it wuz dem uh mee Vito. it wuz duh OK Corral in der. i wuz defendin myzelf. i cudduh been killed."

"But you went there of your own volition."

Paulie's frown deepened. "it wuz wuk. Tuld yuh, Vito, i'm uh zoldier. Diz iz wut i doo. Gud killz people ull duh time, dunee?"

"Are you comparing yourself to God now?"

Paulie shrank back.

"Getouduh 'ere Vito. i ain comparin myzel tuh Gud. i'm uh soldier, datz ull i'm zayin. Uh soldier, fightin uh wuh."

...you've just confessed to mass murder...

"Yuh wuntmore stuf like dat? Huh?"

Father Rozzi didn't reply.

Paulie was eager to continue, he could tell. It was bordering on boasting now.

The futility of it washed over Father Rozzi once again, but he fought against the feeling.

...I'm a priest, remember, I'm a priest...

"Gud wunnuh no 'bout uh zizzy i tuk up wid in duh

can? Howzbout dat kinduh ding?"

"A sissy in the can?"

Paulie was grinning cheekily.

"Are you saying you had sex with a man in prison?"

Paulie's face instantly dropped into a furious sneer, his energy shifting alarmingly. He became deathly still, something malignant oozing from him like invisible smoke.

Father Rozzi almost flinched back from the force of it.

...hey choir boy...

It flashed through his thoughts, with a tremor of nerves, that he was alone with Paulie.

All alone in there...

...no...
...remember, this is my church, my confessional...

"i ain nuh fag," Paulie muttered through clenched teeth.

"But didn't you just say – "

"i ain nevur had sex widduh man."

"I'm confused then Paulie."

"Uh zizzy ain nuh man," Paulie snapped angrily.

"You committed sodomy?"

Paulie's eyebrows jumped. "Wut?"

He glared at Father Rozzi, his eyes narrowing to slits.

...wutchuh brin dat kid tuh hide behine fur...

"Don't answer if you don't want to."

Paulie considered for a moment. "Fuckin' uh zizzy ain duh zame az zodmy Vito."

"Uh, I can't agree Paulie."

"Heh, heh. Yur cunfuzed Vito. Zee, uh zizzy ain nuh man. She wuh lipztick, an pantyhoze, an uh bra. i azkyuh, dat soun likurh-man tuh yoo?" He jabbed his big thumb into his chest, defensively announcing, "i tuk her undermi wing inder. Dey'd eatun her 'live in dat bear pit iffin it wuzzun fuh mee."

He paused for a moment, then boasted, "Yuh no how many brudz i banged?"

"Is that something to be proud of?"

Although he didn't reply, Paulie's arched eyebrows indicated he obviously thought it was.

He pointed a manicured nail at Father Rozzi.

"Lungz itz cler Vito, i ain nuh fag. Yuh gettzuh free pazz fur goin widduh zizzy induh can."

"Well, you don't get a pass in here," Father Rozzi snapped.

Consternation stormed Paulie's face.

He mumbled. "Huh. Diz frum uh guy wearz uh dress."

"Pardon?"

Louder now. "Yurruh tuff crowd Vito. Yuh ain nevur bin induh can. Yuh dun un'ztan wut itz like bein induh can."

"Well – "

"Der ain nuh wimmin inder!"

"Priests *are* human, Paulie."

"Huh. Tellin' mee. i ain evun goin der."

"What do you mean?"

He leaned in, leering at Father Rozzi.

"Yuh tuk tuh mee bout zodmy. Wut bout yoo lut, hah?"

"My lot?"

"Priezt."

"What do you mean?"

Paulie shrugged, his mouth puckering with satisfaction.

"Juz zayinz ull." His face reverted to innocence. "Hay, i ain zayin nuthin bout yoo."

"What do you mean?"

"Like yoo dunno, cummon."

"Tell me."

"Wut, ull diz abuze goin on, wid yoo priezt bangin' choirboyz."

Paulie stared at Father Rozzi as if vindicated, a Cheshire cat grin gleaming on his mouth.

"Wut bout dat?"

Father Rozzi said nothing.

"i ain nevur bang'd nuh choirboyz.

Wut bout dem priezt, an duh Vatigun cov'rin it-up fur 'earz, huh, lettinum go doo it zumwerz elze. Wut bout dat?"

"That has happened, you're right. There are some bad apples, even in the priesthood."

Paulie snorted contemptuously. "Bad applz, huh. Dat wutyuh cullit?"

"Evil exists everywhere, even in the Church. We all have to be vigilant against evil."

"Deze priezt – priezt hah! – fiddlin' wid choirboyz – wut bout dem?"

"What about them?"

"i no moze dem priezt doin dat abuze iz mickz and spicz. Dey ain Italianz."

"Please don't – "

Paulie held up his hand, demanding to know, "Dey goin tuh hell, dem priezt, doin dat?"

"Yes, they are, of course."

Paulie looked sceptical. "Huh. i bet wunnadem cumtuh zee yuh, confezzd tuh fiddlin wid choirboyz, yuh'd give'im uh free pazz."

"A free pass? I don't even know what that is."

"He'd gettoff."

"What do you mean, get off?"

"Don tellmee yuh don zcratch each oth'rz backz, yoo priezt. Go tuh see each othur, confezz ull duh vile shit yuh been uptuh, give um uh few hail Maryz tuh say, an wipe duh slate cleen."

"It isn't like that Paulie. Not at all."

Paulie was having none of it. "Guttuhbee uh perk. Guttuhbee."

"It doesn't work that way."

"Guttuhbee."

"A priest isn't God."

"Ullz i'm azkin iz fur duh zame favur yuh'd giv dem kiddi fiddlerz."

Father Rozzi was annoyed, and confused, "Favour?"

"i don wunnuh go tuh hell Vito."

"It isn't up to me whether you go to hell or not Paulie."

"Wutt-i-guttuh doo den?"

"I've told you. Bring yourself closer to God."

"How?"

"Confess, and – "

Exasperated, Paulie snapped, "i juz dundat."

"But I'm concerned about what you said Paulie."

"Wut?"

"About taking your own life."

Paulie waved a dismissive hand. "Dat? Bettur danduh ultunutive."

"You realize what that is? It's a mortal sin."

...one of many...

"Ain gunnuh endup like Dom." After a pause, Paulie made a suggestion, "Howzbout diz? if yuh cant give mee ablution, yur helpz mee gett'in duh pergtree. Atleaze doo dat much, huh."

Father Rozzi again felt the futility of the conversation wash over him.

...remember I'm a priest...

"Get you into purgatory?"

"Datz duh way it wukz, ain it. Wutz a million yurz in pergtree? Like uh day dun here. Yuh addz up ull yur mortul sinz, multipli dat by fifty, add up yur venul sinz, mutipli dem by twenti five – i cundoo dat standin' on my head. Ain dat duh way it wukz wid purgtree Vito?"

"Where did you hear that?"

Paulie was disappointed, "Ain dat duh way it wukz?"

"I can't get you into purgatory, or heaven."

"Huh."

"Only you can."

"How?"

After a pause, he answered, "I don't hear any contrition from you Paulie."

Paulie waved a weary hand, "Dat contrition ding 'gain." A vexed look came over his face. "Bout dem Culumbianz?"

"Do you feel contrition about anything you've done?"

A look of confusion crossed his features. "Wut i dun?"

…wutchuh bring dat kid, tuh hide behine fur…

"To confess without contrition is like washing laundry without water."

Paulie snorted sarcastically, "Juh getdat outtuh uh fuhtune cookie?"

"I'm saying, it's in your hands, not mine. I'm only a guide."

Paulie stared.

After a charged silence, he mumbled ominously,

"Zo, yuh wun doo mee diz favur?"

"I'm trying to tell you, I can't. I can help, but there's a lot of work to do."

"Wutt wuk?"

…I'm a priest…

"On you."

"Wutt am i, uh patio now?"

Conspiratorially, with a little nod, Paulie suddenly leaned in closer to the partition.

"Howz'bout tuh nuw ruff?"

Father Rozzi was puzzled, "A new roof?"

"Yeh. i'll pay. Howz'bout dat? Give mee uh numbur."

Father Rozzi laughed gently, shaking his head. "You

can't purchase forgiveness Paulie. I'd be neglectful of my responsibilities in here if I wasn't honest with you."

Paulie, frowning, sat back again.

"So, yuh wun doo nuthin."

...'wutchuh bring dat kid tuh hide behine fur'...
...Vito could see it coming...
...Paulie's Sr's eyes narrow and narrow to vicious slits...
...peering at Vito's father like a snake about to strike its prey...

"I'll do anything in my power to help, but I can only do so much."

"Tort dat wuz wutt yuh wonn-ed. Mee confezzin ull diz stuf."

"It isn't just the confessing. It's about atonement, reflection on your sins."

Paulie looked disgusted. "Zo, yuh ain doo'n nuttin.

i ain gunnuh fugget diz Vito. Here? i ain gunnuh fugget diz."

...I'm a priest now...

"Will you pray with me Paulie?"

Paulie flinched as if he'd been slapped. "Huh? Pray? Wudduh yuh kiddin me?"

"Don't underestimate the power of prayer."

"Datz Sunday scool stuf."

"Prayer is our link with God."

...a sneer comes over Paulie Sr's face as, suddenly, with

an animal snarl, he launches himself at Vito's father...

...Vito's father is holding up the ripped birthday shirt, distracted...

...Paulie Sr snatches the shirt out of his father's hand...

...Vito smells stale sweat and other unpleasant odours as a big belly in a white vest bumps his face...

...'IT'S DUH FUTBULL SEASUN', Paulie Sr yells over his head, 'AN YUH BODDERIN' ME WID SUM SHERT'...

...Vito is pushed back, either by his father or Paulie Sr, or by accident, and glances up to see the look of shock and surprise on his father's face as Paulie Sr wraps the shirt around his neck, pulls it tight, and yanks him off his feet...

...Vito's father grabs the larger mans' wrists to no avail as he is propelled across the hallway, his feet kicking at air, and is slammed into the door of the apartment opposite, shaking the walls...

...pinned there, his legs kicking, Vito's father's face turns crimson as he is choked...

...'its-duh-futbull-seasun', snarls Paulie Sr through gritted teeth...

...Vito watches, icy, bewildered panic pulsing through his veins at the sight of his father's assault...

...'heh heh'...

...Vito hears the familiar chuckle behind him and quickly glances over his shoulder at his neighbours' doorway...

...half hidden in the shadows, between the door and the frame, is the pale, familiar face, grinning, watching with enjoyment, Paulie...

...'heh, heh, wuttuh dink bout dat choir boy, heh, heh'...

...the ghostly, grinning face recedes and vanishes back into the darkness of the apartment interior...

...Paulie Sr drops Vito's father to the floor with a crash...

...'get back tuh your linen truck, an don knok on my dor gain, yuh know wuts gud fur yuh'...

...Paulie Sr struts back to his door flashing a white buttock as he yanks up his boxer shorts and slams the door closed behind him...

...Vito's father, in a heap on the floor, pulls the shirt loose from his neck, his hair unkempt, his face red, choking for breath...

...their eyes meet...

...Vito will never forget the desolate look in his father's watery eyes; that his son has witnessed his shame...

...later that night, through the wall of his bedroom, Vito hears his father crying...

"This *is* a church," Father Rozzi snapped irritably.

Paulie pulled a face, waved a dismissive hand in the air.

"Lemme azz gain, yuh gunnuh doo mee diz favur uh nutt Vito?"

"No."

Paulie's furious face suddenly thrust itself close to the lattice partition.

"Yuh juz made duh big mizztake Vito." He nodded in disappointment. "Sum pal. Tort miy uld pal Vito wud sutt mee out. Come ull diz wayz juz tuh zee yuh. Hoo wuzzit had yuh bak bak den, in dat bear pit wee grew up in? Mee, datz who. Aftuh ull i dun fur yoo. Now i know, huh. Well, wutch yuh bak miy frend. i dun care if yuh uh priezt or nutt. Yuh on miy shit lizt."

"Are you threatening me Paulie?"

"Cull it wutt yuh wunt."

"In a church?"

Paulie's face pressed up to the partition, his face resembling a goblin. "Pa wuz ulwayz tellin' mee, 'why can yuh bee muh like Vito nex door, Vito's gunnuh bee a priest, Vito goes tuh church, Vito'z in duh choir, Vito duz diz, Vito duz dat,' Beetin' mee widuh belt an tellin' mee he wishes he cud swap uz aroun'." His voice cracked with emotion. "Miy own Pa, telling mee dat. Miy own Pa. Dat hee wunted yoo fur uh sun, an nut mee. Yuh stole miy Pa frum mee."

…what?…

"Gut sickuh hearin yuh name. Vito, Vito, fuckin Vito. Well, i gave yuh uh chance tuh redeem yuhzelf tuhday Vito. Yuh blewit."

"Paulie -"

Paulie counted off on his fingers, "An i'm takin' bak duh *Gabagool*, duh *pammagiano*, duh *olive oil,* an duh *shooz*. All-uh-vit. i ain givin gifz tuh nuh Judaz."

"Judas?"

"An iff miy carz bin scratch'd bi any deze spickz an niggerz in diz rat hole yuh live in," his big finger stabbed the air at Father Rozzi, "i'm huldin' yuh rezpozible."

Paulie's face loomed close again, his nose touching the partition, his musky scent overpowering, "Yuh ulwayz wuz an asshole Vito. Ulwayz runnin frum duh wuld. Alwayz runnin' intuh St Elzear's likuh pussi."

Father Rozzi couldn't help himself, "Running from you usually."

Paulie's face pulled back in surprise.

Then he nodded, a knowing grin blooming over a wagging, warning finger.

"Wutch yuh bak frum now-on. Wutch yuh bak Vito."

…I'm a priest, remember…

Bending, Paulie picked up the gift bag, and ducked toward the curtain of the confessional.

Father Rozzi called out, "Come and see me after you'd had the results of your biopsy."

Paulie turned, his dead eyes drilling into Father Rozzi's one last time.

He snorted with disdain, "Fuhgeddaboudit."

Then he darted out of the confessional, leaving only his cologne lingering in the air.

Tense, Father Rozzi listened, half expecting Paulie's hand to burst through the curtain and grab him.

He was relieved to hear Paulie clumping away through the pews; then the main door to the street bang closed.

He slumped, a relieved, loud whoosh of breath escaping from his lungs.

Only after swiping off his glasses and rubbing his eyes did he realize he was covered with a thick sheen of perspiration.

He wiped a shaking palm across his dribbling forehead.

His heart was pounding.

He sat quite still for some time, trying to calm himself down.

Father Rozzi meant what he said about Paulie coming back.

But Vito was quaking.

He hoped he'd never see Paulie Gambini Jr again.

...*never*...

God forgive me, he thought, God forgive me.

Don't talk about your semen in front of my friends.

Thirty years Fred Kray had been a black cabbie and now this.

He snapped the newspaper irritably and folded the page over.

They'd won. He couldn't believe it, but they had. They'd won.

Uber had won the case.

The judge had ruled their app was legal in London.

What a fuckin' idiot.

He snorted as he read it.

The judge had ruled that- Fred Kray read it again, to be sure, but still didn't understand it – *'while the smartphone using the app may be essential to enable the calculation of fares, that did not make it a device for calculating fares.'*

"Fuckin' idiot," he muttered. "Fuckin' idiot. What ah fuckin' idiot."

He shook his head and threw the paper down in disgust.

Fred Kray would never have predicted it. Never would have guessed that technology could have any debilitating impact on his life. Let alone threaten his livelihood. Or endanger black cabs. One of the reasons he'd become a cabbie in the first place was because he thought it was a Teflon profession. He thought he'd be immune to recessions, layoffs, closures, redundancies, cuts and austerity…

Thought he'd be protected from all that malarkey.

Now the sanctuary of his cab was being jeopardised.

And by what?

The bloody internet. By some app. A fuckin' app!

He'd never even *heard* of an app a year or two ago, for christ's sake.

"Widiculous," he mumbled to himself, "fuckin' widiculous."

The seat creaked as he shifted his ample bulk reaching down for his tuck box. He balanced the plastic Tupperware on his bulging belly and peeled off the lid. The overpowering aroma of onion and meat escaped from the box, filling the cab.

He sat, gazing out into the dark, empty street, chewing his salt beef sandwich. Pleased his wife, Lena, had put plenty of Dijon mustard on this time. 'Don't skimp onna mustud,' he'd told her. 'It ain't wationed, is it?'

He wasn't even sure what it meant, losing this court case. It was a dark cloud hanging over all their futures. The Licensed Taxi Drivers Association was launching an immediate appeal. But would it make any difference?

What if the doom mongers *were* right, and black cabs disappeared from the streets of London? He still had at least ten years before retiring. What if The Knowledge was redundant now?

What if Fred Kray was an endangered species?

He just couldn't believe black cabs would disappear from the streets of London. No. No way. Worst case scenario, they'd keep a few around for tourists, like beefeaters and red phone boxes. Or maybe there'd be Uber black cabs.

Can you imagine? God forbid!

He finished the sandwich, crumpled the cling film into a ball and dropped it into the tuckbox. (He hated clutter in his cab). He frowned down into the plastic tub. Lena had put an apple and an orange in there, but no crisps.

Bloody 'ell. Not again.

It was part of her ongoing campaign to get him eating healthier food.

Tutting, he picked up the apple, changed his mind, put it back, and picked up the orange instead. Juice dripped from his chubby fingers as he peeled it. The sweet aroma of citrus freshened the stale, beef sandwich air.

He stared into the empty street, shoving a segment of orange into his mouth.

Uber. Fuckin' wankers!

When Fred Kray recalled his struggle with The Knowledge, how he'd sweated over it, and then almost failed despite all his gargantuan effort. All the study, all that time, all the focus…his stomach churned in panic just at the memory of it. How stressed he'd been taking the exams. And now… now this Uber lot comes along, not one of 'em, not a single one of 'em, having put in the work, or the study, or the sweat, or the time.

Wankers!

Opening the window a crack, he let in the chilly night air. After he'd eaten the orange, he wiped his hands with some wet wipes and dropped them into the tuck box alongside the peel, sealing them inside with the lid.

He picked up the paper again, scanned the story one more time, and with a disgusted snort, folded it neatly and slipped it into his bag alongside his tuckbox.

He shifted sideways and let out a loud fart, then

clamped a stick of chewing gum between his teeth. The dry stick quickly morphed into a soft, minty glob in his mouth as he chewed.

The cab shuddered to life as he twisted the ignition key.

He pulled out into the empty street and felt the familiar, soothing power of the vehicle vibrating under him.

As he scanned the passing houses, he recalled the area before it was gentrified, when it was a dump around here. Now these big houses were worth millions. He cruised around the cul de sac, and noticed up ahead a young couple coming out of a front door, clambering frantically down one of the stoops.

Fred Kray's keen eyes observed them.

The frowning woman was black, beautiful, and looked like a model. She was wearing a long, dark purple dress, black leather boots, and a black leather jacket, a little black bag shining over her shoulder. He was lanky, white, slovenly, slouching along behind her with his hands deep in the pockets of his scruffy, faded jeans, a lopsided grin plastered on his face. His blond hair cut in what Fred called a boy band hairstyle. She turned and snapped something at him angrily, then turned her back on him again and resumed her brisk stride.

She spotted the cab and darted between two parked cars into the road, waving her hand. Fred Kray slowed down and pulled to a stop next to her.

She leaned into his window. "Patshull Road, Kentish Town," she told him. He nodded. She clambered into the cab and slammed the door. He yanked down the meter. The door opened again and the man jumped in after her.

"For God's sake," he exclaimed breathlessly, shaking his head, pulling the door closed and slumping back opposite her. She twisted away from him, folding her arms. Fred Kray waited a few moments, watching them in the rear view mirror, before deciding everything was okay.

Lovers tiff, by the looks of things. Just a lovers tiff. He'd seen hundreds of 'em.

He drove off.

"Got an 'lectwic chwair in your place, mate?" he asked.

The man perked up, meeting Fred's eyes in the rear view mirror, a smile re-appearing on his lips.

"Hah? Pardon?"

"Got an 'lectwic chwair at home mate?" Fred asked again.

The man laughed. "Do I have an electric chair at home?"

"Yeah. 'Ave ya?"

"No. No I haven't, strangely enough."

"Pity."

"Why?"

"Cos if ya 'did mate, yah coulda stwapped Lawd Justice Ouseley intwoo it and shot a few million volts thwough 'im."

The man laughed again. He sounded posh. "Who's that then?"

"'Oo's that? I'll tell you 'oo that is mate, some ponce inna wig 'oo wantsta depwive black cab dwivers of their livleyhood, that's 'oo."

"Why would he want to do that?"

"Pwogwess, appawently mate. If that's your idea of pwogwess. 'Aven't ya 'eard 'bout this app?"

"What app?"

"This app these uber dwivers use."

"No."

"No? Not 'eard 'bout this app?"

The man shook his head, amused. "No." He glanced at the woman. "You heard about this app Mel?"

She ignored him, staring out of the window.

The strong aroma of alcohol and cannabis drifted into Fred Kray's nostrils.

"Not 'eard 'bout this app?"

"No," the man shook his head. "What app?"

"Not 'eard 'bout these uber dwivers?"

"Oh. Um, vaguely. Some new company, isn't it?"

"You could call 'em that. Bunch of vultures I call 'em mate. Not one of 'em done The Knowledge. Not a single one of 'em."

"Oh, right," the man responded, bemused, glancing at the woman.

"All the sweatin' I done over The Knowledge, mate. Now this lot comes along and opewate without putting in the time. Diabolical liberty I call it mate. Diabolical liberty."

"Oh, right." He glanced at the woman again.

"I mean, if you get in a cab, mate, you wanna know the dwiver knows where e's goin, don't cha."

"Yes, I suppose I do, yes." He glanced at the woman again.

Fred Kray could tell his punter wasn't interested.

"Couwse ya do mate. Well, thanks to this Lawd Justice Ouseley, that ain't gonna be the case much longa, 'e 'as 'is way."

"Sorry to hear that."

"An' you wanna pay pwoper, don't cha?"

"Sounds terrible," the man answered, glancing at his girlfriend.

Fred could hear sarcasm in the voice. Fair enough. What did this punter care about Uber? He had other things on his mind besides Uber.

The man suddenly jerked forward, grinning, pointing a finger at Fred Kray's displayed I.D. badge.

He sounded very drunk now. "Whoa! Fred Kray. Wahay! Are you related to Ronnie and Reggie?"

"If I 'ad a pound for evwy time someone's asked that, mate, I'd be wich."

He looked at his girlfriend again. "Fred Kray," he said to her, giggling, trying to win her interest.

She stared out the window, ignoring him.

"An' in answer to ya question mate, no, I'm not welated to Wonnie and Weggie Kway. Got nuffin against 'em, mate, nuffin against them, god west their souls. Worse people wound than them, fwar's I'm concerned. But no welation. No welation at all."

"That's a shame."

"Why's that, mate?"

"Oh, I don't know." The man smiled foolishly, caught off guard. "No reason. No reason."

"Like me to be welated to Wonnie and Weggie, would ya?"

"Well, no. No."

"Like me to wegale ya wiv tales of East End cwiminality? That it mate?"

"God no. Not at all. No."

"Sowwy ta disappoint ya mate. No welation. No welation at all. Me name's Kway and I'm an east end boy, but I've worked 'ard all me life. 'An I pay me taxes. No cwiminals in my family. Not that I got anythin' 'gainst Wonnie and Weggie, as I say. Nuffin' at all."

"No offence."

"None taken mate. None taken."

The man glanced at his girlfriend again.

"Like to sic Wonnie and Weggie on 'nese Uber lot. Get 'em to sort it."

"It was just the name," the man said apologetically.

"Pwoud of that name. Pwoud I am. East End bworn and bwed. But Wonnie and Weggie ain't even distant cousins. No cwiminal escapades to welate, 'fwaid mate."

"Thank god for that," the man laughed, trying to make a joke of it.

"No cwiminal skulldugawy, 'fwaid mate."

"Thank god," he laughed again.

"The weal cwiminals innis countwy are in Westminster, ask me anyway, mate."

The man eyes glazed over. "Yes. Yes. You're absolutely right there."

"Fink they pay taxes? All o' the ones' they should be? What they get away wivs cwiminal. Cwiminal mate. Cwiminal. Selling off alla council 'ouses so workin' class people got nowhere ta live. While they get us taxpayers ta pay for their bleedin' patio furniture. Cwiminal, mate. Cwiminal."

Fred Kray slowed at an intersection, stopped, his indicator clicking, watching for a gap in the traffic.

"Alright Mel?" the man asked his girlfriend eagerly, reaching over and grasping her knee.

She sighed heavily, pushed his hand off her leg, and all without taking her eyes away from the window.

He looked at his rejected hand. "Are we going back to yours or mine?" he asked optimistically.

"*I'm* going back tuh mine. I don't care where yur going," she snapped, still not looking at him.

She had a fairly neutral accent, Fred noted, but there was a hint of the north in there. Yorkshire, Fred guessed. Possibly Yorkshire. (It was a game Fred liked to play, pinpointing people's accents). Or was it Lancashire? It was so hard to tell them apart. Impossible, in fact, even if natives of those counties might say otherwise. Many in his cab had maintained they could.

"Oh, come on. What's this for?" the man asked innocently.

As for him, he was public schoolboy all the way, Fred was sure. They had their own county, that lot.

She swivelled to face him. "What's this for? Are you joking?" she asked, glaring.

He answered dismissively, "Because of that stupid dinner party?"

Fred Kray knew when it was time to keep his mouth shut.

"Stupid dinner party?" she repeated angrily. "That's what it was tuh you, was it? A stupid dinner party? Yuh know, those people are friends of mine."

"Well…" the man said sceptically.

"What's that mean? What'd mean, well?"

"Well. They're work friends. Not real friends are they?"

"What?"

"They're work friends."

"Not real friends?"

"You only know them from work."

"What difference does that make?" she asked irritably.

"Just saying. They aren't real friends."

"Not real friends?"

"That's right."

"So, you can't have friends yuv met at work?"

"Well, yes, but – I dunno. Not really. You never see work friends outside work do you?"

"Oh really? Where duh you think we've just been?"

"Yeah, well…"

"I consider them tuh be friends."

"What, even that waxwork?"

"Waxwork? Oh, you mean Mr Mehta? Mr Mehta's gonna be my *boss* next year."

"Oh, yeah, the promotion," he snorted.

"That's right, yeah, the promotion."

"Sucking up to the boss."

"That's right. Sucking up to the boss. That's what tonight was all about, sucking up to the boss. So what?" she answered defensively.

"*Mr* Mehta. You know you called him Mr Mehta all evening. *Mr* Mehta. *Mr* Mehta this, *Mrs* Mehta that. Don't they have first names?"

"So what?"

He put on her voice, mocking her, "Would you like this Mr Mehta. Would you like that Mr Mehta. Can I wipe your arse Mrs Mehta. Can I give you a hand job, *Mr* Mehta."

"It's called being polite. Mr and Mrs Mehta were the hosts."

He blew a raspberry. "The hosts. So what?"

"You just don't have a clue, do you, Jeff?"

"What does that mean?"

She snapped angrily, "Some of us have tuh work for a living."

He threw his hands up in the air. "Oh right. That old chestnut. I thought that would get mentioned. Your favourite topic, hah."

"Yuv got some cheek talking 'bout work friends. What would you know about work friends anyway? Yuv never bloody worked."

"Do me a favour."

"We don't all sponge off our family."

"What?"

"You heard."

"I don't *sponge* off my family."

"They support yuh, though, don't they?"

"Of course my family don't support me," he snapped defensively.

"Sure they don't. Keep tellin' yourself that," she shot back sarcastically.

"I *earn* that money."

She snorted. "Earn it 'ow?"

"I manage those properties."

She laughed, shaking her head. "Yur delusional. Delusional. Yuh couldn't manage a daisy in a plant pot."

He pulled a face. "Yeah, well, whatever that means."

"Yuh don't lift a finger. Yuh live in that flat o' yours for nuthin'. An' on top o' that yuh charge that friend o' yours rent for livin' there and pocket the money he gives yuh for yuhself."

"Yeah. That's right. Because I'm his landlord."

She laughed mockingly. "Landlord," she repeated with disdain. "Your not a' landlord Jeff."

"I am."

"If yuh say so. Your family don't even know about him living there, duh they?"

"So what's any of that have to do with this stupid dinner party?"

"What's it got to do with it? Everything! It's about your attitude, Jeff. You don't pay bills, you don't pay rent. It's all handed to you on a plate. You're such a baby."

Jeff's mouth twisted in resentment.

"Didn't notice you complaining when I took you on holiday twice this year. Three times if you include that weekend in Prague. Didn't notice you complaining about my money then."

"So what," she answered petulantly.

"Yes, exactly, yes, so what."

"That's nothing to do with this."

"Isn't it? You're just attacking me for no reason."

"No reason," she exclaimed in shock, "My god, I've never been so embarrassed in my life."

"What do you mean?"

"Did you have to show up at Mr Mehta's tripping on magic mushrooms and reeking of skunk?"

He laughed out loud.

"It was a party, wasn't it," he said, trying to make a joke of it.

"It was a *dinner* party, not a rave," she hissed coldly.

"Can you imagine Mr and Mrs Mehta at a rave?"

She ignored the comment. "And I especially asked you *not* to be late. Why are you always late? We'd already finished eating by the time you got there. And I asked you to dress up nice as well. Make an effort I said. Remember?

Make an effort. Why'd you have to show up looking like Worzel bloody Gummidge?"

He tutted, offended. "Worzel Gummidge?"

"And when you do finally decide to make an appearance, you show up reeking of alcohol and skunk."

He laughed again.

"What's funny?" she asked icily, staring at him.

"Hark at Mary Poppins here," he answered, pulling a derisory face.

It was her turn to shake her head.

"Why did you have to take magic mushrooms?" she asked. "*Today*? I mean, why? Why today of all days?"

"I didn't realize it was an audience with the Queen."

"Why today?" she persisted.

He shrugged. "Rupert came around."

She tutted, rolling her eyes. "Rupert?" She repeated the name with loathing. "Rupert."

"Yes, Rupert."

"Well say no more. Rupert. I should have known."

"What's wrong with Rupert?"

"What's right with Rupert, more like?"

"You've never liked Rupert, have you?"

"Oh, can yuh tell?" she answered sarcastically.

"He's alright," Jeff said in defence of his friend, seeming to shrink a little into the seat.

"He's a racist twerp, for starters."

"He's not racist," Jeff bristled. "He is *not* racist."

"Thinks I'm your bit o' rough, dunt he?"

"Don't be ridiculous."

"Mind you, so duh rest of yuh family."

He shook his head energetically. "That's outrageous.

Absolutely, outrageous."

"Is it though? Is it though Jeff?"

"Fucking right it is. My family *are not* racist."

"Interesting you'd say that Jeff."

He was caught off guard. "What?"

"Cos I never said they were. I said they thought I was your bit o' rough, not that they were racist."

"What?"

"I never said they were."

"Right," he snapped.

"Not all o' them, anyway."

It was his turn to swivel away from her, staring out the window, his jaw clenched tight.

"What about your Uncle James?"

He'd been expecting it. "Here we go," he muttered.

"What about yuh Uncle James that time at that swanky banquet?"

He tutted, shaking his head. "That was just that one time. That one thing," he muttered, folding his arms, "that one person. And no one in my family has ever liked him, anyway. No one. Everyone thinks Uncle James is a prat. Everyone's always thought so. Don't judge my family based on his behaviour."

"Didn't say anythin' though, did yuh Jeff."

"What was I supposed to say?"

"Neither did anyone else in yuh family."

"What were we supposed to say?"

"Tell him what a prat he is maybe. If that's what yuh all think. Or pull him aside and tell him what he said was inappropriate."

"That would have probably made things even worse."

"So what? At least yuh'd 'ave said something Jeff. 'Ow'd think I felt, having him say that?"

"Not again?" he muttered.

"Goin 'round table doin eeny meeny miny mo, catch a nigger by the toe, and as he says the word nigger, he looks me straight in the eye and grins."

"He's a prat. I told you, he's a prat," Jeff protested shrilly, sinking deeper into the seat.

"Didn't say nuthin though, did yuh Jeff. Yuh uncle called me a nigger. Yuh didn't say anything."

Jeff squirmed in his seat. "He did not call you an n – what's that got to do with this stupid dinner party tonight?"

"Cos yuh let me down that night, an' yuh've let me down tonight as well."

"Oh fuck's sake," Jeff grumbled.

"Yeah, fuck's sake, that's right Jeff. You took the words out of my mouth. Fuck sakes."

"You on the rag tonight, or what?"

She shot him a contemptuous look.

"Don't try tuh sound working class Jeff, it dunt suit yuh."

He laughed mockingly. "Hark at Oliver Twist here. Look at that big house you grew up in."

"My family aren't aristocrats though, are they?"

He shook his head and snorted. "Yes, well, let's not talk about your family. They're all perfect, aren't they?"

They fell into a tense silence, twisting away from each other. She stared out of her window, her arms tightly folded. He stared out of his, shaking his head slowly and continuously, a look of disbelief on his face.

"Rupert," Mel muttered with derision. "Good old Rupert. Rupert dunt work either, does he?"

He gave her a sharp look.

"He's seen me through a lot of rough times," he snapped earnestly.

"Rough times? Yuh mean when yuh were choking on your silver spoon at Oxford. Couldn't find enough chocolate biscuits for one of yuh midnight feasts?"

He sighed. "Talk about other people being a bigot. And it was Harrow, as I've told you many, many times, not Oxford. Harrow."

"Rupert comes round and you just *have* to take some magic mushrooms?"

"Well, it's that time of year, isn't it?"

"What time of year's that?"

"Well, magic mushroom time."

"Magic mushroom time," she repeated, incredulous. "How old are you again Jeff?"

His voice hardened. "Old enough Mel."

She grunted disagreement.

"Mel, you're making a big deal about nothing. Rupert just popped up from Hastings. He was out foraging at four o' clock this morning. I had to be sociable, didn't I? We just made some mushroom tea, god."

"That's what yur did today, is it? Took magic mushrooms, smoked skunk, and got drunk?"

He shrugged a so what shrug. "What are you, my mother?"

"Couldn't just say, no, could yuh?"

"The mushrooms had worn off by the time I came around anyway."

She laughed in derision. "You think so? You came in door babbling like a loon Jeff. Yuh brought whole party to a standstill."

He huffed. "Livened it up more like."

"Party were doin alright by itself Jeff, believe it or not, without your inebriated ramblings."

"What do need me there for then?"

"Cos yur me boyfriend. Invite were for both of us."

"What are you complaining about then? I came, didn't I?"

"Wish yuh hadn't bothered now."

"No pleasing you, is there Mel?"

"I'm not hard tuh please Jeff. Really I'm not. I just don't think Mrs Mehta wanted to hear about how yuh use your semen for hair gel."

He burst out laughing. "Oh yes. I forgot about that."

She stared at him coldly. "Yuh think that's appropriate dinner party conversation, duh yuh Jeff?"

He laughed again.

"Would yuh talk like that at one of yuh families swanky get togethers?"

"Of course."

"Don't think so. Don't think yuh would."

"I was just joking. I can't believe none of them has seen, 'There's Something About Mary.' That's all it was. She asked me about my hair. Fuck's sake."

"Don't talk about your semen in front of my friends," she hissed at him.

He shot back irritably, "Listen, I didn't do or say anything tonight that I wouldn't do or say at a dinner party with my own family."

"Oh come on Jeff. Pull the other one," she snapped sceptically. "Would yuh talk about how you like women with big nipples in front of yuh family?"

He laughed. "Of course."

"And asking Mr Mehta if he drinks his own urine first thing in the morning?"

He laughed again. "I was just asking him about Ayurvedic medicine."

"Or how I make you wear crotchless boxer shorts?"

"Can't I make a joke?"

"And would you sit down at the table with your own family and roll yourself a spliff. Just pulled out your tin and sat there rolling a dooby. Mr Mehta was horrified."

He laughed again.

"None of this is funny Jeff," she informed him icily.

"Oh come on Mel."

"Would yuh do that in front of your family Jeff? Would yuh? In front of your Mum? In front of your Uncle James?"

"Oh god. Not him again."

"These aren't the kind of people you do that in front of Jeff. You were too off your face to even notice."

"Notice what?"

"Mr Mehta's reaction."

"I offered him some, didn't I?"

She tutted. "Some people just don't approve, Jeff. Don't yuh get it? It's Mr Mehta's home. They don't do that kind of thing. It's Mr Mehta's home."

"How could I forget," he mumbled. He threw up his hands and shook them. "Mr Mehta's home, Mr Mehta's home, Mr Mehta's home…," he sang, turning it into a ditty, before dropping his hands and falling into a silent scowl. "Mr Mehta's home" he mumbled ominously.

"I didn't know where tuh look."

"I went and smoked it by the open window didn't I?"

Mel took a deep breath. "When Mrs Mehta said, if you must smoke that, please smoke it by the window, she was actually asking you *not* to smoke it at all."

"She didn't say."

"*If. If* you must smoke it, Jeff. Understand? If. *If* you must smoke it. *If*? Meaning, don't. Meaning, don't smoke it."

He wasn't having it. "Well, she didn't say."

"She did say Jeff. She said it politely."

He sighed.

"Wouldn't do that in your Mum's place, would yuh? That's the point."

"Oh, well, I'm sorry I embarrassed you."

"Yuh did embarrass me Jeff. And I don't believe yuh are sorry."

He shrugged indifferently.

"Oh god," she groaned sadly. "You just don't have a clue."

"Oh, shut up," he snapped angrily.

She snapped back furiously. "Don't tell me to shut up."

"Well don't patronise me Mel."

She shook her head. "I really don't know if there's a future for us Jeff."

He looked at her, startled. "What?"

"We just live in different worlds. Tonight's made that obvious."

"Oh? Has it?"

"Don't yuh think?"

"I think you're making a big deal about nothing." He pleaded. "Come on Mel?"

"Tonight's the final straw."

"Meaning what?"

"Meaning; there's no future for us, Jeff."

He stared at her. She looked away and stared out of the window.

"We've always known we're from different worlds Mel. Right from the start."

"I know. I didn't think it mattered. Now I'm realizing it does."

There was something in her tone.

His attitude softened. "Look, I'm sorry about tonight."

"So am I." After a pause, she added, "but I'm glad as well."

"What do you mean?"

"It's overdue."

"What?"

"This."

There was a long pause. He frowned at her.

"Are you serious?" he asked at last.

"Long overdue Jeff."

"Maybe you shouldn't be so judgemental Mel."

"I'm not being judgemental. I'm just facing facts, that's all. Facing facts Jeff."

"You know, you used to be a lot of fun in the old days. But these days?" He made a derogatory sound. "These days…" He let the words hang there, as if it was self explanatory.

"There yuh go then Jeff."

"I've never pretended to be anything I'm not Mel."

"You've got no ambition Jeff."

"Oh god. Now you sound just like my mother."

"God forbid," she muttered in horror.

He snapped his eyes onto her. "You don't like my family, you don't like my friends. You don't like my lifestyle. I'm fed up with having to apologise for everything I do in my life. It's getting to be a real bore."

"And we all know how much yuh hate being bored, don't we Jeff," she answered sarcastically.

He laughed in frustration. "Okay. I can see this is pointless. This is going nowhere. You're heading back to yours, right Mel?"

"That's right Jeff."

"I'll go back to mine then."

"Yuh do that. Go back and see Rupert. Take some more magic mushrooms."

"You know, I almost brought Rupert with me tonight."

She was appalled. "I hope you're joking?"

"No."

"Well, why not go the whole hog and invite your Uncle James as well?"

"Wahay! Him again."

After a pause, she added, spitefully, "I think there would have been too many brown people around the table for Rupert or your Uncle's liking."

He was disgusted. "Oh! That's it."

He leaned forward and tapped on the glass. "Let me out here will you please Fred."

"Awight mate."

Fred Kray looked for a space to pull over and slowed down.

"Thank you for being absolutely obnoxious company tonight Mel."

"Same here," she answered, her arms folded, staring out of the window, refusing to meet his eye.

Fred pulled over and stopped. Jeff quickly clambered out and slammed the door. He melted into the pedestrian traffic and was gone.

"Got an 'lectwic chwair in your place luv?" Fred asked as he pulled back out into traffic.

"No," she answered, "I *don't*."

She said it in such a tone that Fred Kray never said another word to her.

But when he dropped her off in Kentish Town, she gave him a big tip.

More than the toff boyfriend would have given.

Fred was sure of that.

HESTER CLUTTERS' WAITING ROOM

Hester Clutter watched in surprise as the nigger entered the waiting room and pushed the door closed behind him on the lashing rain.

She glanced down at her daughter, Mary-Ann, intending to show her how to talk to the coloured folk. Set an example. Show her how to best clear up the boys' confusion.

Hester Clutter cleared her throat loudly. Everyone glanced up. Her daughter tore her eyes away from the funny papers she was reading.

Mary-Ann followed her mother's gaze, and saw him. She sat up stiffly, folding her cartoons, and shot an irritable look at her mother.

"What's that nigger doin' in here?" she asked her mother loudly.

That was exactly what Hester Clutter *didn't* want to hear. She didn't like such outbursts. She tapped her daughters' knuckle twice with her finger. Mary-Ann glanced up at the sharp touch of her mothers' disapproval.

That was *not* how to talk to them. Hester Clutter was a devout Christian woman, after all. She gave her daughter a vexed look. Treat everyone with Christian charity. That was Hester's attitude. Yes, even the niggers. Some folks thought it wasn't right, but that was her way.

That was just her way.

She glanced at the other two people sitting in the small waiting room; an immaculately attired, small, frail old man wearing pince-nez, who had lowered his newspaper, and was frowning at the interloper.

And a young woman sat at the far end with a large suitcase at her feet, eyes wide with alarm at the newcomers' entrance.

Hester Clutter glanced back at the nigger again.

He was a soldier.

A bag was draped over his shoulder. He shifted it and let it drop to the ground with a loud thwack. It was soaking and dripped onto the floor. A small puddle swelled at its' base.

He was wearing a long coat over his uniform, which trickled rain. There were sergeants' stripes on both arms. He took a little cap off his head and shook it, sending drops of water flying into the air. Some of the drops spotted Hester Clutters' dress. His left hand was encased in a soiled white cast, and above his right eye were stitches under little white strips. Under the left eye was a healing, but still raw scar.

He must have been wounded, she thought, wounded over there in the war.

"But that nigger ain't supposed to be in here," Mary-Ann protested to her mother.

Hester noticed the black soldier lean his soggy bag against the seat and cast an angry look at Mary-Ann. He stepped over and stood directly in front of her, glaring down, towering over her. He was big, this boy. Real big. What her husband would call prime bull nigger. Mary-Ann recoiled back against the wall, pulling as far away from him as she could, eyes popping in confusion. She threw a frightened glance at her mother.

"I – AIN'T – NO – NIGGER!"

Their shock bounced silently off the waiting room walls.

The coloured boy turned and looked at each of them, his glare a challenge. His eyes came to rest again on Mary-Ann.

"Hear me girl? I ain't NO NIGGER."

With a sneer of contempt at Hester, he turned away. He went back to the bench and sat next to his bag, shaking rain off his sleeves.

Directly above his head, a sign proclaimed:

'WHITES ONLY!'

Not far from that sign, another stated:

'NO COLOREDS ALLOWED!'

Hester Clutter trembled; her heart pounded.

She'd never seen anything like it. As the Lord was her witness – she'd never heard of such an occurrence before.

Never.

She cleared her throat loudly, too stunned to think clearly for a moment.

A nigger! Talking to her Mary-Ann like that?

A nigger boy.

Oh good Lord. Oh sweet Jesus! It was lucky her husband, Clovis, wasn't with them. If he'd heard it…

What would he think when she told him about it later; oh Lord, Clovis already thought they were getting too big for their britches.

"Mama," Mary-Ann croaked in distress.

Hester glanced at her poor Mary-Ann, on the brink of tears. She grasped her hand and squeezed it.

"Mama?"

Mary-Ann's eyes were filling.

"Don't fret honey. Now don't you fret yourself," Hester told her daughter soothingly, patting her hand.

"But Mama," Mary-Ann sobbed.

Hester glanced quickly at the others.

The old man was just staring at the nigger, frowning, his newspaper folded in his lap. Oh, he looked mighty put out, *but he weren't doin nuthin.*

The young woman was staring too, shocked as the rest of them. But no one uttered a word. Not a word.

Hester Clutter fixed her eyes back on the coloured boy.

He was still shaking rain off himself, ignoring them. The boy had some sass. She'd give him that. Some sass this nigger.

Hester believed in treating them with Christian charity, but as Clovis was always saying, where will it end? Where will it all end?

She glanced at the old man again, waiting on him to say something. But he only sat there, silently glaring. Glaring was all well and good, but got folks nowhere. What was wrong with the old fool?

She cleared her throat again.

Well, someone had to say something.

"Boy," she said firmly.

The nigger soldier glanced over at her.

"Ain't no *boy*, lady," he hissed.

"Son," she said, "can't you read the signs?"

The soldier grinned. "Can read just fine lady. Got mysel' an education over there servin' Uncle Sam. Yes Mam, I can read jus fine. Sign say waitin' room don't it?"

"Other signs in here too," she pointed out.

The soldier sighed. "Lady, I jus wanna sit down and

shelter from the storm blowin' out there. That's all I want. Same's you."

"Other signs in here too," she repeated.

"I don't read them other signs so good lady," the soldier answered mockingly, "all I know is, dis ah waitiin' room, an I'm awaitin.'"

"This a waitin' room for whites only," she told him, "whites only," she emphasized.

"I am white lady," he answered with a grin.

"You ain't white," Mary-Ann snapped indignantly.

"I'm white as you sugar; jus' been over in the tropics. Got me a mean suntan on this lilly white ass o'mine."

"You ain't no white man," Mary-Ann turned to her mother. "He ain't no white man."

"Sure I is."

Hester Clutter had never seen such sass in a nigger. Lord almighty.

"Boy," she said, "you ain't supposed to be in here."

"Sure I is. And like I told you lady, I ain't no boy."

"You best read them signs again son."

"I read 'em," he answered.

"You had your fun, boy," an old, reedy voice sounded out, "best collect your things and be on your way."

They all glanced at the old man.

Finally, Hester Clutter thought, he's spoken out. Better after the fires' started than when the barn's burned down.

The soldier glared at the old man.

"You best get nigger!"

Hester Clutter, smiling smugly, waited for the intruder to pick up his bag and leave.

But he didn't move. He just stared at the old man.

239

She'd never seen such an expression on a niggers' face before.

The old man glared belligerently back at him.

Outside, the rain lashed the roof as the wind roared.

"Old man," the soldier said finally, his voice slicing through the tension like a hot knife through cheese, "you an ignorant old fool."

Hester Clutters' heart skipped. Oh my Lord!

"You best get while the goings good boy," the old man seethed.

The soldier gave the old man another long spell of vigilance.

Hester listened to the heavy drumming of rain on the roof.

"Know where I been old man? Know where I been dis last three year?"

"I don't care where you been nigger," the old man snapped.

"I bin to hell and back. Un'stan old man?"

"I don't care where you been nigger!"

"I put on dis uniform to fight for my country. Bin over there fightin' for you old man." He glanced at Hester Clutter. "Bin fightin for you lady. Bin fightin' for your little girl there. Bin fightin' so she can grow up free an' happy. That's what I bin told anyhows."

Fightin' for Mary-Ann?

"You recognise the uniform?" He held his arms out. "You musta seen it before."

"You best get nigger."

"Dis my country old man." He glanced at Hester Clutter. "Dis my country lady. Un'stan?"

"This *ain't* your country boy, and it sure as hell ain't your waitin' room."

"How come I'm wearin' dis uniform pops? Don't it mean nothin'?"

"Not to me."

"There ain't anudder waitin' room old man."

"That's your problem nigger."

The furious soldier jumped to his feet and planted himself in front of the old man.

"I – AIN'T – NO – NIGGER!" he bellowed down at him. "Un'stan' old man. I – AIN'T – NO – NIGGER! I'm a sergeant in the United States Army. I ain't no nigger and I ain't no boy. You got that straight?"

The old man quivered, but his gaze never faltered, staring up into the eyes of the soldier.

"I was twenty years younger, I'd drag you outside and give you a horse whipping," the old man hissed up at him, his reedy voice cracking with emotion.

The black boy glared down at him; then his face broke into a gap toothed grin.

"You got some vinegar old man, I'll give you that. We coulda used some of that piss and vinegar over there old man. We coulda sure used you over there all right."

He swung around, chuckling, and returned to his seat.

The old man sat shaking with silent fury.

Hester tapped Mary-Ann's hand. "Best go get Franklin," she told her.

Mary-Ann shot a derisory look at the soldier. "You ain't no white man!" she snapped at him, before hurrying out the door.

A loud whoosh of storm sounded loudly from the open

doorway for a few moments, before it banged closed and a hush returned.

"Now where she goin'?" the soldier asked quietly.

No one answered.

"Ah hah," he grinned, a few minutes later, when Mary-Ann stepped into the waiting room behind Franklin.

Franklin was retiring in six months. He was dragging a leg under his crooked back. Been working that station as long as Hester could remember; he didn't have his cap on; his grey hair was dishevelled. His uniform looked crumpled too; with an egg stain on the lapel.

Looked to Hester like he'd been napping.

"There he is," Mary-Ann exclaimed accusingly, pointing.

Franklin blinked sleepily at the soldier.

"Oh, now come on boy," he exclaimed in sleepy exasperation, "you know you ain't supposed to be in here. Scoot boy." He clapped his hands to emphasize the point. "Scoot on outta here boy." He clapped his hands again. The slap echoed off the walls.

The soldier boy scanned the room theatrically, his eyes searching the corners. "There a dog in here?" he asked.

"This nigger been causin' trouble Franklin," the old man told him shrilly.

"Been gettin' real fresh with my Mary-Ann," Hester added softly.

Franklin glanced from them back to the soldier, his crooked back straightening with indignation.

"That right boy?"

"I jus' shelterin' from the storm, same's everyone else."

"You cain't shelter in here boy, you know that. What the hell you thinkin'?"

"Ain't lookin' for no trouble."

"That nigger a trouble maker," the old man snapped, "called me an old fool."

"That right boy?"

Hester cleared her throat in assent.

Franklin glanced at the young woman in the corner.

"He been stirrin' trouble," she murmured.

Franklin put a hand on his hip, staring at the soldier, and scratched his tousled grey hair.

"What'ya doin' 'bout it Franklin?" the old man asked.

"You call Jeremiah an old fool, boy?"

"Dis uniform mean nuthin' to you either, old timer?"

Franklin's face creased into bewilderment.

"Uniform?"

"Dis uniform mean nuthin' to you?"

"What's uniforms got to do with it?"

"Does dis uniform mean nuthin' to none o'you people?"

"Nigger in a uniform don't mean nuthin'" Jeremiah spat.

"Uniforms don't change nuthin' boy," Franklin told him.

"I looks like a boy to you?"

"Told us he wus a white man," Mary-Ann snapped.

"White man?" Franklin scoffed, "you as black as coal, boy."

"Jus' shelterin' from the storm. All I'm doin. Can't a soldier servin' his country shelter from a storm?"

"This whites only in here, boy."

"There ain't anudder waitin' room, Dis the only one."

"That's cos' we a real small station here. But there ain't no mixing son. You know that. Ain't no mixing."

"Throw that nigger outta here Franklin," the old man protested loudly.

"What in tarnation you think I'm doin' Jeremiah,"

Franklin replied irritably.

"I ain't movin," the soldier stated calmly.

Franklin couldn't believe his ears. "What you say boy?"

"I ain't movin. An I ain't no boy, old man. Don't call me that 'gain."

Franklin stared at him, scowling, looking him up and down, trying to comprehend what he was dealing with.

"You know what you doin' son?" he asked.

"I ain't movin. Jus' shelterin' from the storm. Figure after everythin' I bin through should at least be able to do that in the country I bin fightin' for."

"Told you he was a trouble maker" Jeremiah hissed in fury. "What ya doin' bout it?"

"It ain't right," Hester put in, "him bein' in here with Mary-Ann. Ain't right."

"Gonna ask you one more time son," Franklin drawled, "Get yourself outta here fore' things get outta hand."

"Jus shelterin' from the storm. Jus shelterin' from the storm. Ain't no cause for folks to get het up."

"I don't make the rules, son," Franklin told him.

"Get that nigger outta here Franklin," the old man demanded, exasperated.

"Come on son, I'm askin' you one last time. Just carry yourself on outta here and we'll forget all 'bout it."

"Ain't movin."

Franklin looked him up and down again; he was so goddamn big.

"Ain't movin."

The utterance was so final Franklin knew there was only one thing he could do.

"Well, I'm gonna have to call me the sheriff," he said,

hoping the mention of the sheriff might change things.

"Ain't movin."

"Alright then. You folks is just gonna have to put up with it 'till I get the sheriff."

"Well, damn well hurry it the fuck up," old Jeremiah snarled.

Mary-Ann's mouth formed a shocked O as she glanced at her mother. Hester shot an appealing look to Franklin.

Franklin noticed. "Remember there's a child here Jeremiah. You might wanna tame that tongue a little."

"This woulda never happened in my day," the old man seethed, "never in my day."

With a final look of despair at the soldier, Franklin shook his head and sighed.

"Have it your way son. Sheriff ain't gonna be happy bein' dragged out here for this."

Franklin left, muttering to himself.

Mary-Ann, who had been on her feet throughout the exchange, returned to her seat next to her mother; feeling exposed standing in the middle of the room while everyone else was sitting.

"Sure is a stormy night," the soldier observed, "a stormy, stormy night."

"Shame on you," the young woman in the corner uttered softly.

They all looked at her. She was staring at the soldier.

The soldier shook his head, smiling, staring back at her. "Shame on you sister. Shame on all of you."

"Just wait 'till the sheriff gets here nigger," Jeremiah warned.

"There's a war on old man. Just don't seem to realize I'm on your side."

"If I was twenty years younger boy…" the old man replied ominously.

"Why don't you leave before the sheriff gets here?" Hester suggested, trying to calm the waters.

"Ain't goin' nowhere lady. I earned this seat. You people don't un'stan. I *earned* this seat."

The old man snorted in derision. "Doin' what? Cleanin' latrines?"

The soldier grinned at him, shaking his head. And just replied, "no old man."

They waited.

The storm was getting worse. The wind slammed into the walls; the downpour pounded on the roof.

It seemed an age before the door finally opened again.

"What the hell Franklin!"

The sheriff entered first, his plastic mac dripping and shining, water cascading from the brim of his wide hat.

"Call me out on a night like this for nuthin'?"

"Ain't nuhin. This nigger won't leave. These folks wannim outta here."

The sheriff took off his hat and shook water off it, scanning the room, scowling and shaking his head.

"Goddamn it. I been dragged out here on a night like this cos o' you boy?" the sheriff barked at the soldier.

The soldier leaned forward, resting his elbows on his knees.

"Jus' shelt'rin' from the storm. Ain' done nuthin'."

"Goddamn it," the sheriff cursed.

"This nigger a troublemaker," old Jeremiah told him. "Get him the hell outta here sheriff."

"Been real fresh with my Mary-Ann," Hester Clutter added, "real fresh."

"That right boy?" the sheriff asked.

"Ain' done nuthin' sheriff. Ain' done nuthin'. An I ain' no boy. I'm a sergeant in the United States Army."

"Hear that? Told you this nigger was a troublemaker sheriff."

Mary-Ann spoke up. "Told us he wus a white man."

Hester had her say. "Ain't right him bein' in here with Mary-Ann."

The sheriff took another look around the waiting room, sighing.

"Tellin' me I'm missin' my supper cos o' this. I was just sittin' down to a lovely fish supper. Caught 'em myself just this morning. Nuthin' like fresh fish cooked straight off the hook."

"Throw this nigger on outta here an' you can get back to your goddamn fish supper," Jeremiah almost howled. "What the hells' wrong with you? Get this nigger outta here."

The sheriff tilted his head and stared severely at Jeremiah. "Now you just rein in your temper Jeremiah. I'm the one should be vexed, getting' called out on this fools' errand."

"What else was I supposed to do?" Franklin complained.

"Do your goddamn job," Jeremiah retorted to the sheriff. "This would never have happened in my day. Never in my day."

The sheriff looked at the soldier. "What about it boy? You stirred up a hornets nest in here. How about just takin' yourself on outta here an' lettin' me get back to my wife and supper?"

"You *askin'* him?" Jeremiah whined in derision. "Just throw him the hell outta here!"

"I need you to tell me how to do my job, Jeremiah, I'll ask. Just don't be holdin' your breath."

"In my day that nigger be danglin' from a rope by now."

"Ain't no lynchings happenin' while I'm sheriff," he snapped at the old man. "Times have changed Jeremiah."

"Not for the better. Not for the better. You let these niggers run amok round here."

The soldier shook his head and grunted.

"Could you find it in yourself to be real quiet for five minutes Jeremiah. You're gratin' on my good nature," the sheriff informed him.

"Just get that nigger outta here," the old man replied angrily.

"Give me a chance, that's just what I'll do. That's just what I'll do."

The sheriff looked the trouble over again. Took in the uniform, the wounds, the stripes, the defiance. Realized he wasn't dealing with some run of the mill nigger.

"Been overseas boy?" he asked.

"Yep," the soldier answered.

"Been through the grinder over there by the looks of it."

"Bin servin' my country sheriff."

"That's good son. All credit to ya."

"Figured dis uniform might mean something to people back here. Figured they might see more than jus' a nigger when they see this uniform." After a second, he added, "guess I wus wrong."

"Well, these folks just stuck in their ways son. Just stuck in their ways."

"This uniform mean nuthin' to you neither?"

The sheriff pondered the question a moment. "My boys' over there," he told him. "Been over there more than a year now. Nearly a year an' a half. Wearin' the same uniform as you son."

"Huh," the soldier answered, "bet he could shelter from a storm without havin' threats of bein' lynched thrown in his face, hah?"

The sheriff glanced at Jeremiah with a frown. "Ain't no lynchings goin' on round here son."

Jeremiah lurched forward angrily, pointing his rolled up paper. "What them signs say on the wall? Whites only. That's what them signs say. Whites only. You plan to talk him on outta here sheriff?"

"This boys' been fightin' for Uncle Sam Jeremiah," the sheriff answered. "Been over there fightin' with my boy and lots of other good men."

"What them signs say?" Jeremiah screeched, pointing at the wall.

"Just simmer on down Jeremiah," the sheriff held a hand out, "simmer on down."

"What the hells' wrong with you?" the old man fumed.

"He ain't supposed to be in here sheriff," Franklin put in, "these people got a right."

The sheriff shot Franklin an irritated look. "Don't lecture me on rights, Franklin."

Franklin shrugged and kept his mouth shut.

Hester said, "He gave my Mary-Ann real sass, sheriff; scared her half to death."

"Said he wus a white man," Mary-Ann added.

The sheriff looked the room over again; rested his eyes on the soldier. "You see how it is, son."

"Drag that nigger outta here," Jeremiah screeched.

The soldier flared up. "I ain' no nigger old man. My name's Atticus Trent. I'm a sergeant in the United States

Army. I bin fightin' three an' a half years for my country, an for people like you. I ain' no nigger."

"Read them signs nigger," the old man shot back.

"I'm gonna throw *you* on outta here you not careful, Jeremiah," the sheriff warned him.

"Well, that figures," the old man snarled in disgust. "Why don't you throw us all out an' leave the nigger here? That about your speed sheriff? Get on back to that fish supper then, hah?"

The sheriff shook his head in consternation, a little grin on his face.

"I ain' saying nothin'," Franklin murmured, saying a whole lot.

The sheriff addressed the soldier again. "You see how it is son."

"I earned this seat, sheriff. I earned it", Atticus Trent said through gritted teeth.

The sheriff sighed. Everyone was watching him, waiting on him. He put his hands on his hips, pondering the situation.

Hester Clutter wondered what he was waiting on? He should have thrown that sassy nigger out as soon as she told him about him getting fresh with Mary-Ann.

"You see how it is son," the sheriff said regretfully.

"You gonna throw me outta here sheriff?"

The sheriff held his hands out helplessly, shrugging.

"You gonna throw me outta here," Atticus Trent asked again, disappointed.

"These people want you out of here son," he replied wearily.

Atticus grabbed his bag and rummaged around inside.

"Never see the like," old Jeremiah snorted, revolted.

The soldier took something out of his bag. "Tell me somethin' sheriff."

"If I can son."

"Wus won'drin whether dis gonna mean somethin' back here or not. Guess I'm gonna find out."

"What's that?"

"The United States government gave me this. Said I'd served my country with honour and bravery. Wid distinction."

Atticus stood up and approached the sheriff, holding out a decorative square box. He stopped, opened the box, and showed the sheriff the contents. The sheriff looked down into the box, eyebrows arching as he took in the sight. "Well now," he commented.

Hester Clutter could tell whatever was in the box had impressed the sheriff. He took a step back almost, she thought, in awe.

"A General pinned this to my chest sheriff. Said I'd served my country wid distinction. Said he wished there were more like me."

"That's a hell of a thing son. A hell of a thing. You should be real proud son. Real proud."

"I should be. How come I ain't?" Atticus Trent asked accusingly.

The sheriff met his eye. They locked eyes for some moments until the sheriff glanced away.

"Congressional Medal of Honor is somethin' to be proud of. Somethin' to be proud of for sure," the sheriff declared, addressing the remark to everyone in the room.

"Don't earn me a seat in here though, do it sheriff?" Atticus Trent asked bitterly.

The sheriff took a step back, shaking his head. "Well now son," he drawled, all out of sorts.

"Old man," Atticus snapped, stepping up to Jeremiah, holding the medal out for him to see, "you think I got dis cleaning latrines?"

Jeremiah peered at the medal thrust under his nose, his lip quivering.

"That's a hell of a thing," the sheriff declared loudly, "a hell of a thing for any man to have."

"Some piece of tin given by a yankee General to a nigger don't mean nothin' to me," Jeremiah hissed.

"Coulda sure used that piss and vinegar over there old man," Atticus answered, "sure could."

The soldier swung around and thrust the box under Franklin's nose. "Mean anythin' to you pops?"

Franklin peered at it, perplexed. "What you want me to say?" he asked, glancing at the sheriff.

"They don't understan' son," the sheriff told Atticus Trent.

Atticus went to Hester Clutter and showed her; showed it to Mary-Ann too. Hester, bewildered, stared down at the medal. Mary-Ann pulled a mocking face.

"Mean anythin' to you? Either of you?" he asked.

"Like wut?" Mary-Ann asked.

"Real nice," Hester said, not knowing what else to say, glancing at the sheriff, wondering when the heck he was going to ask that nigger to get out of there.

Atticus watched them intently, then swung around and moved toward the young woman in the corner.

She shrieked softly and held her hands out, shaking her head frantically as he approached. "No. No. Please don't come near me," she pleaded.

Atticus halted after a few steps, a pained look on his face, as if he'd been slapped.

"I ain't gonna hurt you lady," he said, bewildered. "Jus showin' you something is all."

"Get the hell away from her nigger," Jeremiah shouted.

Atticus turned and looked at the old man, then at the sheriff.

"You see how it is son," the sheriff told him sadly.

Atticus stood there, the medal clutched uselessly in his hand, despair on his face.

"So this means nuthin'?" he murmured.

"It sure does son. It sure does. Just not to these people," the sheriff answered.

Atticus gazed down at the medal with a stunned expression. "So it don't mean nuthin," he said, almost to himself.

"Jesus H. Christ," Jeremiah snarled, "you gonna get this nigger outta here sheriff."

"You see how it is son," the sheriff said again.

Atticus looked at each one of them, one by one, nodding.

"I shoulda known," he said quietly, "guess I wus forgettin' where I am."

He replaced the lid on the box, went over to his bag, and pushed the medal back inside. He turned back and addressed them, a strained smile on his lips.

"Guess I ain' welcome."

"You guessed right nigger," Jeremiah snapped.

"You ain' people," Atticus declared, and turned his back on them.

He picked up his bag and swung it over his shoulder, went across to the door, and left the waiting room.

Mary-Ann blew a raspberry at his disappearing back.

Hester tapped her hand and shook her head.

"God almighty," Jeremiah declared in exasperation and relief.

Hester breathed a sigh of relief too. Wait until Clovis heard about it. What was he going to say about *this?* As the Lord was her witness, she'd never seen anything like it in her life. Clovis was going to be furious.

"Never in my day," Jeremiah declared, shaking his head, "never in my day."

"Okay then," Franklin nodded, dragging his crooked back to the door, muttering to himself as he left.

"If that's progress, you can keep it," Jeremiah said, snapping his newspaper open on his lap.

"You okay now honey?" Hester Clutter asked Mary-Ann.

"Wait 'till I tell Pa," she pouted, and resumed reading her funny papers.

The sheriff looked them over. "Well, you folks done yourselves real proud today," he told them.

They all stared at him.

"Thank you sheriff," Hester Clutter remarked, a little bewildered by his comment.

"Thank you sheriff," the young woman in the corner added.

He nodded slowly, gave them a final look, and after a gruff, "Evenin'," disappeared out of the door.

"Hm. Now I seen it all," Jeremiah snorted, "a nigger lovin' sheriff." He shook his head in dismay.

The incident had shaken Hester Clutter.

She sat listening to the storm lacerating the walls and roof.

The room suddenly felt stuffy; she got to her feet to stretch her legs, crossed to the door, and opened it.

A blast of rain and wind buffeted her, lifting her dress, making her step back.

Lightening flashed across the dark, rumbling sky.

She saw the nigger in the flashes, standing on the platform, his coat flapping in the wind. The downpour was soaking him. He was staring at something held in his hand. It looked like that box he'd been flashing at everybody; that medal thing of his. He was just standing, gazing down at it.

Suddenly, she saw him lurch back, raise his arm high, and hurl the box into the wet, stormy darkness.

He stood staring after it, motionless as a statue, the storm swirling around him, appearing and disappearing in the flashes of lightning.

Hester Clutter couldn't believe it.

She stepped back into the waiting room and closed the door.

One minute that niggers' flaunting that medal thing of his like it's something important, like it mean somethin', next he's tossing it away like garbage.

Wait until Clovis heard about it.

Like he was always saying, these niggers don't appreciate nothin'.

This book is printed on paper from sustainable sources managed under the Forest Stewardship Council (FSC) scheme.

It has been printed in the UK to reduce transportation miles and their impact upon the environment.

For every new title that Troubador publishes, we plant a tree to offset CO_2, partnering with the More Trees scheme.

MORE TREES
LET'S PLANT A BILLION TREES

For more about how Troubador offsets its environmental impact, see www.troubador.co.uk/sustainability-and-community